I0638142

Sellout

by
Donald Jans

FADE IN:

SUPER: 2009

EXT. TIDE POOL - BIG SUR COAST - MORNING

A cocky SEA OTTER floats on his back enjoying the crispness
of his Northern California oasis. The otter seems to smile
to a flying seagull CAWING as he scans the rugged cove. A
powerful wave CRASHES against cement stairs which lead
sharply up a cliff away from their paradise. At the top of
the stairs beyond the golf-green quality grass lies one of
the most incredible MANSIONS of the California coast.

INT. LIVING ROOM - COASTAL MANSION

Rugged and still handsome at (58), OTTO PREMINGER, dressed in
gym shorts and a T-shirt, basks in a leather easy chair in
his incredibly appointed living room. As he ponders the blue
Pacific ocean, a French-American beauty, JEANINE(34), naked
save for a short silk bathrobe, slinks her arms around Otto
from behind.

                    JEANINE
               (mild French accent)
          Good morning master.

Jeanine giggles and kisses his cheek. Otto smiles and looks
ahead, completely satisfied, stroking her arm.

                    JEANINE (cont'd)
          What was that last night?

Jeanine slides into his lap, and kisses him again.

                    OTTO
          The ol' dog still has a few tricks.

Jeanine hikes her eyebrow.

                    JEANINE
          And I didn't even have to get out
          the peanut butter.

Otto smiles, shakes his head and kisses her.

                    JEANINE (cont'd)
          What would his good-in-bedness like
          for breakfast? My crepe suzettes
          are getting really good.

                         OTTO
          Nice to know those private lessons
          with Martha Stewart are finally
          paying off.

Otto pats her butt as she gets up and admires her beautiful
muscular and tanned legs as she exits.

                         JEANINE
          Two $20,000 crepes coming right up.

Jeanine calls out from the kitchen.

                         JEANINE (O.S.) (cont'd)
          Baby, we're out of eggs. Be back
          in a flash.

                         OTTO
          OK.

Keys JINGLE as they are SCRAPED off the counter. The door
SLAMS.

Otto shakes his head and clicks a black BUTTON on his easy
chair. A behemoth PLASMA TV rises from the floor.

Otto clicks on the TV. On the TV, a REPORTER stands in front
of a shocking IMAGE of the smoldering WHITE HOUSE.

The panicked reporter touches his earpiece as he nervously
glances behind himself and details the tragedy.

Otto is speechless and closes his eyes in guilt.

                         NEWSCASTER (ON TELEVISION)
          A radical Arabic off-shoot has
          claimed responsibility for this
          latest heinous attack on American
          soil.

Otto picks up his high tech cordless phone and quickly dials.

INT. DORM ROOM - BERKELEY

Outdoorsy and super-handsome, DUSTIN (18) fumbles for the
phone. Two SURFBOARDS lean against the wall of his pigsty.

                         DUSTIN
               (raggedy morning voice)
          Hello?

                         OTTO
          Dustin, I've got something very
          important to tell you.

INTERCUT AS NEEDED

Dustin grabs for the clock radio. It reads 7:32.

                         DUSTIN
          It's like the middle of the night.

                         OTTO
          This tragedy is all my fault.

                         DUSTIN
          Dude, relax, I'm almost off
          probation.

                         OTTO
          Turn on the TV.

                         DUSTIN
          This is a first.

Dustin fumbles for his remote, but is interrupted by curly
red haired REBECCA (19) who rolls over and lays on Dustin's
chest and caresses him. Dustin is immediately distracted and
looks down at his crotch.

                         REBECCA
                    (whispering)
          Who is it?

                         OTTO (O.S.)
          Son, I'll never forgive myself for
          what I've done. I was only
          thinking of the money.

Off camera, Rebecca is obviously fellating Dustin. He talks
to both of them.

                         DUSTIN
          Which I appreciate very much.

                         OTTO
          Your grandfather would turn over in
          his grave.

Dustin looks down at Rebecca.

                         DUSTIN
          I think he'd be pretty proud.

A CALL WAITING BEEP interrupts.

>   OTTO
>   Hold on Dustin.

>   DUSTIN
>   I'll try.

Dustin sighs in joy, puts the phone near his ear and puts
both hands on her head.

INT. LIVING ROOM

Otto clicks over.

>   OTTO
>   Hello?

>   JACK
>   Otty, they're at it again.

INT. LIVING ROOM - TAHOE REGION

JACK (58), burly and weathered, paces in his massive lodge
that boasts a wall of glass VIEW of the expansive Sierra
forest.

>   JACK
>   Told ya we should have developed
>   gramp's idea.

>   OTTO
>   It's gone too far. We've got to go
>   public.

INTERCUT AS NEEDED

Another call waiting BEEP interrupts their conversation.

>   JACK
>   I've been telling you.

>   OTTO
>   Dustin's on the other line.

Jack realizes he's been hung up on, shrugs, hangs up and
grabs his fishing pole and charges outside.

>   OTTO (cont'd)
>   Dustin, are you there?

INT. DORM ROOM

                    DUSTIN
          (moaning)
    Yeah.

                    OTTO (O.S.)
    What the?

BANG

Rebecca hangs up the phone.

INT. LIVING ROOM - COASTAL MANSION

The wind fluffs the expensive drapes. The continual TV
COVERAGE of the White House disaster ruins the eerie silence.

                    NEWSCASTER (ON TELEVISION)
    An understaffed police force has
    given way to rampant looting in the
    immediate area of the disaster...

INT. KITCHEN

Jeanine enters weighed down by two bags of fresh groceries.

                    JEANINE
          (yelling)
    The raspberries looked beautiful,
    so we are having those instead.

Jeanine continues to unload the groceries, including a fresh
BAG of Peet's COFFEE.

                    JEANINE (cont'd)
    Vous tu encore cafe?

Jeanine walks in the living room, sniffing the open bag of
coffee. She senses something is wrong. She crosses the room
to close the open window near the fluffing drapes. Her
attention is sucked to the news coverage on TV.

                    JEANINE (cont'd)
    Oh my God! Otty, did you see--

She turns around to discover Otto's lifeless figure on the
ground near his chair. The coffee drops and spills
everywhere. She slumps in sobbing tears over his body, and
rocks him back and forth.

She sits upright in a tearful rage, looking at the ceiling.

                         JEANINE (cont'd)
                    (crying and screaming)
          WHY...WHY...WHY.

Her rage turns to hurt.

                         JEANINE (cont'd)
               I'm here to protect you baby.

She caresses his face and slumps over him.

EXT. OCEAN VIEW CEMETERY - CARMEL - DAY

Dustin, dressed in his best black suit wearing Ray-Bans,
struggles to keep himself from crying as he hugs and greets
the throngs of mourners.

FRED (20), an athletic black guy with the latest haircut,
gives him a heartfelt hug.

                         FRED
               It'll be cool Dust.

Dustin nods, but can't speak.

                         FRED (cont'd)
               We'll party and talk it out when
               you're ready.

                         DUSTIN
               Thanks man.

Dustin chokes back his tears.

ERIN (19) an athletic, natural beautiful brunette, hugs
Dustin to temper her own sobs.

                         ERIN
               I'm so sorry.

She continues to hug him. Dustin rests his head on her
shoulder wishing he were alone with her. He can only nod.

Rebecca rudely interrupts the two. Her blood red finger
nails wrap around the back of his neck.

                         REBECCA
               Oh Dustin.

She pulls Dustin towards her and inappropriately sexily
kisses him. Erin looks on in controlled disgust at Rebecca.
Rebecca sneers at Erin and turns Dustin away from her.

Jack approaches Dustin and stands protectively by his other
side. He hands Dustin his handkerchief. Dustin BLOWS his
nose and tries to hand it back. Jack motions "keep it".

Jeanine, ringed by her own group of mourners, looks over to
Dustin wishing she could hug him. Dustin returns her empathy
with a mean glare. Jack steps in front of Dustin.

> JACK
> You're coming up to the mountains
> for a month to get your head
> together.

Dustin looks up to Jack, thankful he has someone he can lean
on. Jack slaps his arm around Dustin's shoulder.

> DUSTIN
> You mean it?

> JACK
> Fishing, clean air, good food...

> DUSTIN
> Thanks Jack.

Rebecca stays near his side, arms crossed, almost bored. She
readjusts her gold chained designer purse. Jeanine walks
over to Dustin. Dustin puts Jack in between them.

> DUSTIN (cont'd)
> Would you get her the fuck away
> from me.

> JEANINE
> Dust...I'm hurting too.

> DUSTIN
> Now you can get all the money you
> wanted right up front.

> JACK
> Dustin, don't talk to her like
> that.

> DUSTIN
> He'd still be alive if it weren't
> for you.

Jack jerks Dustin back behind him.

> JACK
> Jeanine, we'll talk next week.

MATCH CUT: Jack winks at Jeanine.

INT. JACK'S LODGE - LIVING ROOM - TAHOE REGION - AFTERNOON

CLOSE UP: An old photograph of Jack winking.

Dustin and Jack flip through old PICTURES in the massive
timber-beamed room. A near empty WINE BOTTLE sits on the
coffee table in front of the flickering Tahoe-esque river
rock fireplace.

                    DUSTIN
          Man, you guys were so skinny.

                    JACK
          Don't worry, you'll be a fat ass
          just like me one day.

Jack smiles and pats his belly, knowing full well that's he's
no fat ass. He jumps up to the granite counter that
separates the open floor plan from the kitchen. He
effortlessly lifts two cases of wine.

                    DUSTIN
          Mom, was hot! How did dad ever
          work that.

                    JACK
          He was a pretty smooth talker.

                    DUSTIN
          So that's where I got it from.

Dustin smirks at Jack and continues to absorb the photos.

                    JACK
          So, did pops ever tell you who your
          grandfather was?

                    DUSTIN
          No, not much, some inventor dude--

                    JACK
          Or even better, your great grand-
          father?

                    DUSTIN
          They sounded like hard-asses.

Dustin yearns to hear more.

                    JACK
          Died when I was ten, a heart attack
          or something. Or so they say.

                         DUSTIN
              I think you've got the right idea.

Dustin admires his incredible view.

                         JACK
              You really don't know, do you?

                         DUSTIN
              Know what?

Dustin puts the pictures down and stands up.

                         JACK
              Who your grandfa--great grandfather
              was?

                         DUSTIN
              From our stump of a family tree.

Jack throws the now empty wine box at Dustin pointing towards
the waning fire.

                         JACK
              You're all I've got too.

Dustin plops the box on the small fire. It catches
immediately and ROARS. Jack walks up behind him and tosses
the second box. He tussles Dustin's hair.

                         JACK (cont'd)
              How bout what your "inventor dude"
              great gramps did?

                         DUSTIN
              What's the big secret?

                         JACK
              How about that he was so paranoid
              about someone stealing his
              grandson, that no one ever knew he
              was married?

                         DUSTIN
              Full on freak!

                         JACK
              Did you ever learn about Nikola
              Tesla?

                         DUSTIN
              Who's that?

                    JACK
          Your grandfather.

                    DUSTIN
          So.

                    JACK
          So, smarty-pants, we wouldn't have
          electricity or radio without him!
          That's a pretty big SO!

                    DUSTIN
          No way! You are shitting me. Like
          he invented it?!

                    JACK
          All of it.

                    DUSTIN
          I thought it was Edison, and
          Macaroni..Marconi, whatever.

                    JACK
          Nope.

                    DUSTIN
          So that's where Dad got his bacon.

                    JACK
          Sort of, and me, just by being your
          uncle.

                    DUSTIN
          I thought you owned that sporting
          good chain?

                    JACK
          So I wouldn't have to explain every
          5 seconds where my money came from.
          That thing loses money every year.

                    DUSTIN
          Got any more this?

Dustin holds up the empty bottle of wine and purposely BURPS.

                    JACK
          It ain't water ya know. That's
          $275 a bottle. Wholesale.

                    DUSTIN
          You can afford it.

                         JACK
               Follow me.

Jack and Dustin scurry downstairs, arriving at a vault like
door.

INT. HALLWAY

Jack punches a series of numbers in to the KEYPAD. The door
opens with a VACUUM sound. Jack and Dustin enter.

INT. WINE VAULT

                         DUSTIN
               Radical! No teenager is gonna
               steal your wine.

                         JACK
               About 5 million bucks worth.

Jack splays his hand to show the 20,000 bottle wine cellar.

                         JACK (cont'd)
               Temperature controlled of course,
               and lead lined to keep out any
               stray radiation from those pesky
               nuclear bombs.

                         DUSTIN
               They'd mess your whole day up.

Jack grabs a bottle of wine, expertly opens it with a
Screwpull, and provides two clean fresh glasses.

                         JACK
               I know you have the attention span
               of an ant sometimes, so I'll be
               brief.

Dustin swirls and sniffs his wine as Jack goes to his grand
bookshelf and retrieves a massive antique book, "GREAT
INVENTORS".

                         DUSTIN
               Is he in there?

                         JACK
               Nope, he's not the first to get
               screwed out of his credit due.

Jack opens the page to THOMAS EDISON.

                    DUSTIN
               (a la Spicoli)
          I know that dude. So he's not the
          one who invented elect--

                    JACK
          Direct Current, not alternating.

                    DUSTIN
          What's the difference?

                    JACK
          DC...direct current, is like
          batteries. The power can't travel
          far, and in a power plant, it's too
          dangerous, that's Edison.
          Alternating Current, that's your
          gramps. He changed the world.

                    DUSTIN
          I've never even heard of him.

Dustin shakes his head in disbelief.

Jack reaches in to a drawer to retrieve extremely old
PHOTOGRAPHS.

                    JACK
          He was waiting til you were 21 when
          your real trust would kick in.

 Dustin examines a photo of handsome NIKOLA TESLA.

                    DUSTIN
          Bet he got laid a lot.

                    JACK
          He barely had time for that. But
          she understood that.

Jack presents a PHOTOGRAPH of a fair woman in typical
Victorian era dress, standing behind Nikola.

                    JACK (cont'd)
          Meet your great grandmother.

                    DUSTIN
          Gramma had a big bootie.

Jack socks Dustin in the arm.

                    JACK
          Watch it!

Jack presents another well-known PHOTOGRAPH of Nikola, this
time in front of two resistors arcing electricity.

                    JACK (cont'd)
          He worked for Edison when he first
          came here from Serbia.

Dustin grabs the massive inventors BOOK and begins to read.

                    JACK (cont'd)
          It's a well known fact Edison put
          his name on a lot of things he
          didn't invent.

                    DUSTIN
          So Edison stole gramps invention?

                    JACK
          The opposite. Fought to suppress
          it, because it made his obsolete.

                    DUSTIN
          But everyone thinks Edison invented
          it anyway.

                    JACK
          Not everyone. The truth comes out
          eventually, even if it takes 100
          years.

                    DUSTIN
          How'd gramps get his deal out
          there?

                    JACK
          You've heard of Westinghouse?

                    DUSTIN
          Kind of.

                    JACK
          He saw the vision, and knew it was
          the wave of the future. He paid
          gramps a million dollars for it.

                    DUSTIN
          That's it?

                    JACK
          That was a hell of a lot of money
          back then. They harnessed Niagara
          Falls together.

                    DUSTIN
          Damn.

                    JACK
          That's what everyone else said,
          including General Electric backed
          by J.P. Morgan using Direct
          Current.

                    DUSTIN
          Why didn't he just keep it all for
          himself.

                    JACK
          He knew it was bigger than him.
          And he knew if the big boys weren't
          cut in on it, they'd kill it, or
          you. Ever wonder why we still use
          gas and oil?

                    DUSTIN
          It's 7 bucks a gallon!

Jack turns the page to show the invention of the MODEL T.

                    JACK
          Did you know the original Model T
          could run on alcohol?

                    DUSTIN
          So it's the car companies!

                    JACK
          It's bigger than them, or our
          government. It's the powers that
          be. They have to have some way to
          keep us in control.

                    DUSTIN
          Get the fuck out.

                    JACK
          You could have a still in your
          backyard and never buy gas.

Dustin air banjoes and sings the plucking noise a la
"Deliverance".

                    DUSTIN
               (singing)
          Der,der,der,der,der,dur,der,duhr,da

                    JACK
          Just about the time cars were
          becoming all the rage, alcohol was
          being blamed for all America's
          problems.

                    DUSTIN
          Prohibition.

Jack flips a page showing a PICTURE of the Women's Christian
Temperance Union picketing.

                    JACK
          So, some ball-busting Christian
          chicks on parade, whose husbands
          would rather hang around the bar
          than come home, struck a cord with
          the government.

                    DUSTIN
          How'd they convince them?

                    JACK
          They didn't have to. If folks were
          making booze in their back yards,
          there was no way to tax either the
          alcohol to drink, or the alcohol
          used as fuel. Plus it made you
          unproductive.

Dustin takes a big swig of wine.

                    JACK (cont'd)
          Gasoline is difficult to refine. It
          takes big money to pull it out of
          the ground, and bring it to your
          car.

                    DUSTIN
          So that way, only a few people can
          do it.

                    JACK
          You're not so dumb after all. Have
          a look at these.

Jack walks over to a closet and pulls old BLUE PRINTS out of
a large tube. He splays the elaborately drawn prints on the
table. Dustin is puzzled by its round shape, like a bundt
cake, with a Gyroscope-like mechanism in the center.

                    DUSTIN
          What up with this?

                    JACK
          Sustainable non-polluting energy.
          Nuclear fusion.

                    DUSTIN
          Nuclear's not new.

                    JACK
          It's fusion not fission.

                    DUSTIN
          Like I would know the difference.

Dustin is awed by the design.

                    DUSTIN (cont'd)
          How could this NOT be developed!

                    JACK
          Well for one reason, your father
          sold the technology.

                    DUSTIN
          Mine?! To who?

                    JACK
          The Men in black, the government,
          the illuminati, I don't think he
          even he knew.

                    DUSTIN
          How did they know he had it?

                    JACK
          Because he was your grandfather's
          son. And even that was a secret
          for a long time. He was young. He
          didn't know what he had, or how it
          worked. He wanted to make a quick
          buck, or bookoo bucks as the case
          was.

                    DUSTIN
          That was lame.

                    JACK
          You sure are benefitting from it.

                    DUSTIN
          Yeah, I guess.

                    JACK
          It's easy to point fingers when
          you're not in that situation.
                    (MORE)

                    JACK (cont'd)
          You have something...Everyone wants
          it. He just thought they would
          develop it.

Dustin shakes his head, speechless.

                    JACK (cont'd)
          With this, the only use we'd have
          for petroleum is for the Vaseline
          to finally fuck them.

                    DUSTIN
          So it's gotta be the oil companies.

                    JACK
          Not the oil companies. The people
          behind the oil companies. The
          richest families in the world. They
          would lose control.

                    DUSTIN
          Like the Rockefellers?

                    JACK
          Much more secret than that.

                    DUSTIN
          Whoa, all the terrorism stuff...
          you think?

Jack motions Dustin out of the wine vault. They exit.

He pushes the door shut and re-locks the door via the KEYPAD.

INT. HALLWAY

Jack and Dustin head slowly up the stairs.

                    DUSTIN
          Arab fucks.

Dustin gets agitated. The sound of a DOOR OPENING perks both
their eyes.

                    JACK
          Hold on Hitler. That's what they
          want you to think. They are just
          pawns and victims in their game
          too.

LING SUN (35), a super sexy, tall and confident Asian beauty,
strides with 4 bags of groceries.

                    LING SUN
          I heard pawn and victim. You ready
          to lose at chess again so soon?

Jack smirks and raises his eyebrows. He lovingly pulls her
to him and passionately kisses her, relieving her of the
plastic grocery bags. The electricity of their relationship
is evident.

Jack puts the grocery on the floor and irresistibly kisses
her again.

                    JACK
          Dust, meet Ling-Sun.

Dustin looks nervous.

                    DUSTIN
          Dad said your name was Lucy?

Ling pushes Jack away.

                    LING SUN
          Are you cheating on me again?

                    LING SUN (cont'd)
          That's my cheesy American name.
          Dad didn't know what was hip when
          he got off the boat.

Dustin is impressed by her candor.

                    LING SUN (cont'd)
          Hey Dustin, I'm really sorry to
          hear about your dad. He was a
          great guy.

                    DUSTIN
          Thanks.

                    LING SUN
          I hope you stay as long as you
          want.

                    JACK
          Hold on now.

Jack holds on to Ling like a toddler snatching his toy.

                    LING SUN
               (affected Chinese hooker)
          You no worry Mr. Jack, prenty Ling
          Sun for eberyone.

Dustin eats up her irreverence and knows they've made an
instant bond.

>   LING SUN (cont'd)
>   I make you and #1 son berry good
>   dinner now master.

>   DUSTIN
>   I love Chinese food.

>   LING SUN
>   So do I, but tonight you'll eat the
>   best red pepper pasta, ever.

>   JACK
>   She was a model in Milan when I met
>   her.

>   LING SUN
>   Until he rescued me.

She bats her eyes like a starlet and kisses Jack.

>   JACK
>   She had one of those old guy
>   fetishes.

Ling Sun saunters towards the kitchen.

>   DUSTIN
>   (to Jack)
>   Dude, she rocks.

Ling overhears and beams. Jack holds up two fingers.

>   JACK
>   Two Phd's.

>   LING SUN
>   (yelling from kitchen)
>   Don't forget the minor in cock
>   sucking.

Dustin falls off the couch laughing as Ling sachets in wiping
the corner of her mouth holding a beautiful ANTIPASTO TRAY.

>   LING SUN (cont'd)
>   Just in case your brains don't get
>   you a job.

Dustin dives in to the antipasto. Ling sets out crystal wine
glasses. Jack grabs her waist and sits her down on his lap
as she pours the red wine.

Dustin takes a gulp. Ling swirls then sips.

>   DUSTIN
>   Tasty.

Jack examines the bottle.

>   JACK
>   You opened up the Rothschild for
>   the little squirt.

>   LING SUN
>   I'd say it's a pretty special
>   occasion. It's not everyday that I
>   get to meet the...

Jack nods that she can continue.

>   LING SUN (cont'd)
>   Great grandson of Nikola Tesla.

>   DUSTIN
>   You know about him too?

>   LING SUN
>   Pretty amazing guy. I finished up
>   my thesis on alternative energy
>   sources. He was a man out of time.

>   DUSTIN
>   Dad sucked at secrets?

Dustin looks at Jack for what else he's missing.

>   LING SUN
>   That's how I met Jack, during my
>   research.

>   JACK
>   You know how kids talk.

>   LING SUN
>   I'm sure you've got a harem of
>   girls swarming you at Berkeley.

>   DUSTIN
>   Nobody like you.

Dustin flirts.

>   JACK
>   OK, that's it. Touch my girl and
>   you're dead.

Ling and Dustin laugh. Jack jumps into the kitchen to grab a
bottle of Pellegrino.

> LING SUN
> Isn't he romantic? So there's no
> lucky "one".

> DUSTIN
> I've got a couple in rotation. Got
> one coming up tomorrow if that's
> cool.

Ling looks at Jack for his approval.

> JACK
> Barely can stand one night alone
> with me, huh?

Dustin makes an endearing face and turns up both hands.

> JACK (cont'd)
> (Southern redneck)
> If it'll keep you away from my
> woman, bring'em on.

Jack hugs Ling around the waist.

Ling winks at Dustin and laughs at Jack's false jealousy.

EXT. JACK'S LODGE - DAY

Dustin stands with Rebecca at the rear of his '72 topless
Burnt Orange Bronco. She sizes up the lodge exterior. She
sports a black tight sweater, leggings and too many silver
bracelets. Dustin struggles with all her bags.

INT. JACK'S LODGE

Jack and Ling stand together as Rebecca enters first. Dustin
barely gets through the door. Rebecca scans the interior.

> DUSTIN
> (breathless)
> Jack, Ling, meet Rebecca.

> REBECCA
> Dustin's told me so much about you.

Rebecca offers her hand.

> DUSTIN
> I have?

                    LING SUN
          Your room is all ready upstairs.

                    REBECCA
          With Dustin?

Jack looks at Ling, smirking at her pushiness.

                    JACK
          Sure, why not?

                    DUSTIN
          Rebecca's parents are Christian
          fundamentalists.

Rebecca looks at Dustin to stop.

Dustin grabs her things and heads upstairs.

                    JACK
          Why not take Erin down to the boat
          and show her the lake.

                    DUSTIN
          Um, Jack. You know this is
          Rebecca.

Rebecca stares at Dustin in a controlled rage. Dustin grabs
her bags and shrugs his shoulders at Rebecca who turns up the
stairs. Dustin turns and struggles to free his middle finger
to flip off Jack, and playfully mouths "FUCK YOU", nodding
for payback. Jack is proud of his cleverness. Ling shakes
her head and playfully hits Jack on the shoulder.

INT. BEDROOM

Rebecca unpacks her things. Dustin attempts to help.

                    REBECCA
          You told me you two had broken up.

                    DUSTIN
          Well, sort of.

                    REBECCA
          You lied.

                    DUSTIN
          I just don't ditch people. We were
          good friends.

                         REBECCA
                Bet she doesn't know how to do
                this.

Rebecca kisses Dustin. She masterfully slides her hand over
his crotch, leaving him breathless.

Rebecca spanks his tight perfect butt and bites his lower
lip.

INT. KITCHEN

Ling and Jack prepare another gourmet meal.

                         LING SUN
                She seems nice.

                         JACK
                Good in bed maybe, nice? neuh,uh--

                         LING SUN
                What am I?

                         JACK
                Both.

                         LING SUN
                Good answer.

They kiss. The phone RINGS. They remain lip-locked.

                         LING SUN (cont'd)
                Let it go.

                         JACK
                Might be Dustin's lawyer.

Jack grabs the phone.

                         JACK (cont'd)
                Hello? Well, hello Erin. Yes he
                is, one minute.

A devilish grin overtakes Jack.

                         LING SUN
                You're bad.

                         JACK
                     (yelling)
                Hey Dust.

INT. BEDROOM

Dustin is down to his tighty-whities grinding on top of
Rebecca.

> DUSTIN
> (annoyed)
> What!?

> JACK (O.S.)
> Telephone!

> DUSTIN
> I'm busy! Take a message.

> JACK (O.S.)
> It's Erin. She says it's
> important.

Dustin is busted looking in to Rebecca's eyes. He picks up
the phone.

> DUSTIN
> Hey Erin, what's up?

Dustin looks suspiciously at Rebecca and shrugs.

> ERIN (ON TELEPHONE)
> Was I interrupting something?

> DUSTIN
> No nothing.

Rebecca is pissed. She sits upright and buttons her shirt.
Dustin tries to calm her down while still being suave on the
phone.

> DUSTIN (cont'd)
> What was so important?

INT. ERIN'S DORM ROOM

> ERIN
> Nothing, I can call later.

INTERCUT AS NEEDED

> DUSTIN
> Why'd you say it was important?

> ERIN
> I didn't.

                         DUSTIN
                    (under his breath)
          Jack.

                         ERIN
          Look, if you don't want me to come.

                         DUSTIN
          No, it's not that.

Rebecca fumes out of the room.

                         REBECCA
          Liar.

                         ERIN
          Who was that?

                         DUSTIN
          Nobody, I gotta go.

                         ERIN
          Do you still want me to come up
          this weekend?

                         DUSTIN
          Yeah, sounds good.

A call waiting BEEP sounds in Dustin's ear.

                         DUSTIN (cont'd)
          Hey hold on.

                         ERIN
          Just call me later.

Dustin clicks over.

                         DUSTIN
          Hello.

INT. LAWYER'S OFFICE - SAN FRANCISCO

WARD SCOTT (44) impeccably dressed and handsome, talks on the
phone in his opulent office that boasts a commanding view of
the Golden Gate. Judging by the unusual shape and style of
his office, it's obvious he's at the top of the Transamerica
building.

                         WARD
          --we've got a lot to talk about.

                         DUSTIN
          Can't we just do it over the phone?

INTERCUT AS NEEDED

                         WARD
          Too busy to hang out with your
          Uncle Ward? No Dustin, I need your
          actual hands to open some of this
          stuff.

                         DUSTIN
          Oh, all right.

                                             CUT TO:

INT. CONTROL ROOM - UNDISCLOSED LOCATION

The incredibly appointed high tech room is loaded with
computers, screens and inventions we are not yet aware of.
GREELEY (22), clean cut but with a surfer attitude, listens
intently with RAQUEL(23), an intelligent looking attractive
girl. Greeley perks his eyebrows.

                         DUSTIN (O.S.)
          What time?

                         WARD (O.S.)
          How about 11. I'll even validate
          your parking.

Greeley shakes his head to Raquel.

                         GREELEY
          Spoiled rotten snot.

INT. LIVING ROOM - JACK'S LODGE - MORNING

Dustin puts his coffee cup in the sink. Rebecca sits
drinking hers, agitated.

                         REBECCA
                  (whining)
          I just got here.

Rebecca folds her arms like a 5 year old.

                         DUSTIN
          I didn't plan it. He said I've GOT
          to go.

Dustin goes in for a kiss, she turns and gives him her cheek, then coquettishly looks at him.

INT. '75 FORD TRUCK - MORNING

Jack drives Dustin down the mountain road both dressed in nice casual clothes.

>   DUSTIN
>   You know you didn't have to drive
>   me.

A '62 beat up CHEVY TRUCK putters in the distance.

>   JACK
>   You kidding. I've been wanting to
>   see inside this secret box since
>   you were born.

Jack looks in his REAR VIEW MIRROR. He notices a black MERCEDES following them. Dustin wonders what has piqued Jack's attention and turns around to view the sedan.

>   JACK (cont'd)
>   Watch this.

Jack rounds a steep corner and jerks the steering wheel to the right accelerating behind a 6 ft. Juniper bush that leads to an almost invisible narrow gravel road. They continue at a slower speed up the hill to a landing where they can observe the sedan speeding up to search for Jack's vanished truck.

A huge smile takes over Jack's face.

>   JACK (cont'd)
>   (country accent)
>   Mrs. Johnson isn't going to take
>   kindly to the city slickers.

Jack points and chuckles.

The sedan speeds up and rides the bumper of her weathered '62 Chevy truck.

INT. CHEVY TRUCK

CLARA JOHNSON (70) and grizzled, flips the bird to the sedan.

                    CLARA
               (singing)
          Oh, Iiiii'm just a coal, miner's
          dawter....

The sedan tries to pass her. She slows down to annoy them.
As they accelerate and attempt to pass, she swerves in their
path and grins. The two overly clean-cut MEN (30's) both
dressed in dark sunglasses and suits, are confounded.

                    CLARA (cont'd)
          Kiss my ass, city punks.

INT. SEDAN

The passenger side man takes out a silencer from its case.

                    DARK SUIT MAN #1
          Should I take the old bitch out?

                    DARK SUIT MAN #2
          No, not now.

The driver makes a daring move along the shoulder of the
road, finally pulling past Clara.

INT. '75 FORD TRUCK

Jack and Dustin continue up the steep dirt road.

                    DUSTIN
          Who are they?

                    JACK
          My little friends who've been
          following me for years. You'd
          think they'd at least try to drive
          a less noticeable car.

Jack shakes his head and smiles.

                    DUSTIN
          Why?

                    JACK
          Usually I just let them follow, but
          today, I'm not in the mood.

They arrive at a shiny black BELL HELICOPTER.

INT. SEDAN

The two men see the shiny helicopter buzz right over their
heads.

> DARK SUIT MAN #1
> That's him. Damnit.

He bangs the steering wheel. The other man immediately picks
up his space-age phone.

> DARK SUIT MAN #2
> All radio contact lost...in
> helicopter headed for San
> Francisco.

An AERIAL VIEW shows 3 separate helicopter pads on different
hills, 2 with parked helicopters.

INT. WARD'S OFFICE

A big-bosomed secretary, TRIXIE (45), wearing dangling hoop
earrings and a 60's polyester pants suit, opens the door to
greet Jack and Dustin.

> WARD
> Dustin, my boy.

Ward hugs Dustin and smiles.

> JACK
> Where'd you find that?

Dustin moves his eyes to Trixie. Trixie prepares drinks for
the men. Dustin walks to the window and looks down.

Dustin's POV: The city street is marred by signs in store
fronts that read "GOING OUT OF BUSINESS" and "WE GIVE UP".
Dustin sighs and turns around

Trixie delivers the drinks.

> TRIXIE
> Here you go boys.

Trixie closes the door behind her. Ward motions them to sit
down. He hands Dustin a 5"X 7" FRAMED PICTURE of a beautiful
girl in a bikini posing on a dock at Lake Tahoe.

> WARD
> Look at this.

Dustin moves the picture to back and forth and looks behind the high tech FRAME.

                    DUSTIN
          Does she take her clothes off or
          something?

                    WARD
          Push that button on the right.

Dustin complies, there's a CLICK and a WHIR.

Ward takes the frame away.

                    WARD (cont'd)
          It knows your bone structure and
          retina.

                    DUSTIN
          For what?

                    WARD
          To match up with this.

Ward holds a glowing PAD and moves the frame within the pad.

                    WARD (cont'd)
          All when you were a baby. Place
          your palm here.

Dustin is stunned and places his palm over the pad.

                    DUSTIN
          Then what?

                    JACK
          Boy you ask a lot of questions.
          Your dad didn't tell you shit did
          he?

                    DUSTIN
          I guess not.

Ward takes the entire glowing pad and slides it in a slot in the wall.

A DOOR opens in the wall with a SWOOSH.

                    WARD
          Wooo-heee! I've been waiting too
          long to see what's in here! Your
          dad and you were the only ones with
          access.

Ward opens the large 3'X 3' box to find a curious stainless steel OBJECT, most similar to a gyroscope seen from the blueprints at Jack's. Also in the box are VCR TAPES, countless DOCUMENTS and an old PHOTO of Otto and his beautiful mother standing behind 7-year old Dustin who struggles to hold up a string of fish.

                    DUSTIN
          I remember that.

Dustin admires the photo. Jack and Ward gaze over at the picture.

                    DUSTIN (cont'd)
          He said he was too afraid to put
          the worms on a hook.

                    JACK
          Yeah right--

                    DUSTIN
          Well he let me think so. I caught
          all the fish by myself.

                    JACK
          He was very proud of you Dustin.

                    DUSTIN
          That day I remember feeling like I
          could do anything.

Dustin eyes well up with TEARS.

Jack gives Dustin a loving punch in the arm and tussles his hair.

                    JACK
          Sometimes he would start talking
          about you on the phone. I'd go get
          something in the fridge and come
          back and he'd still be talking.

Dustin starts to smile and grabs a VCR TAPE.

                    DUSTIN
          Is this a home movie?

                    WARD
          I was there the day he made it. He
          made me leave the room.

Ward anxiously shoves the tape in the VCR and flips on the modern TV.

ON TV: A jittery picture shows a chair in a seemingly empty room. OTTO sticks his face close up to the lens, appearing much younger.

> OTTO (ON TELEVISION)
> Dustin, is that you? Romper,
> stomper, domper doo, tell me, tell
> me, tell me do.

Otto pretends to look through the camera to Dustin with a curious smile.

Dustin beams.

> OTTO (cont'd)
> So if you're watching this, that
> means I'm either dead as a door
> knob or you and Ward got really
> curious and both worked it out so
> you could see this.

Dustin, Jack and Ward smile and shake their heads at each other.

> OTTO (cont'd)
> Before you get all pissy that I
> only left you 5 million and gave
> the rest to charity. Here's why.

The group moves closer to the screen.

> OTTO (cont'd)
> Dustin, I was weak. I took the path
> of least resistance. Your
> grandfather figured out the needed
> physics to provide sustainable non-
> polluting energy.

Dustin grabs the shape from the box.

> OTTO (cont'd)
> It involves magnetically controlled
> plasma twisted in a toroidal shape,
> that once heated, can stay that way
> for long periods of time.

Dustin looks at Jack confused. Jack looks at his shoes.

> OTTO (cont'd)
> Word traveled fast to the families,
> and this little baby was going to
> ruin their empire.

Jack gives Dustin a "see I told you so" look.

                    OTTO (cont'd)
          Bottom line, your dear old dad sold
          out, instead of finding the right
          people to develop it.

Dustin looks at the ground.

                    OTTO (cont'd)
          So, here's how it works.

                    WARD
          Let's play this one first.

Ward removes the tape and pushes in TAPE #3.

Otto appears older, more recent, fidgeting in the chair,
almost exasperated.

                    OTTO (ON TELEVISION)
          It's me again. Lately I've been
          talking to the families, to try to
          give them their money back. But
          it's too big...too vast.

                    WARD
          He just did this 3 months ago.

                    OTTO
          So I think something is going to
          happen.

They all look at each other.

                    OTTO (cont'd)
          One of the spoiled kids from one of
          the families wants to toss the
          checker board off the table, like
          another 9/11. They say it's going
          to happen in the US.

Dustin looks at an 80's photograph on the wall of New York
City at sunset complete with the intact World Trade Center.

                    OTTO (cont'd)
          I wanted to go public to stop him,
          and they told me they'd stop me if
          I did. Dustin, I love you more
          than anything and if I'm dead, now
          you know why. DO NOT FIGHT THEM.
          Be good to Jeanine. She really
          loves you Dustin.

Otto blows Dustin a macho kiss and winks.

                    OTTO (cont'd)
          Jack, I know you're there too, and
          thanks.

Otto stands up and turns off the camera, leaving a blue
screen.

Ward turns the TV off. Dustin's face is streaked with tears,
his eyes beet red. He wipes his nose with his bare hand.

                    DUSTIN
          Those fuckers! Who are they!?

                    WARD
          Honestly Dustin, I don't know what
          he's talking about.

                    JACK
          Dustin, I do. Let it go.

Jack hugs Dustin. Dustin breaks away.

                    DUSTIN
          No way.

                    JACK
          Dustin, I won't lose you too.

Jack bear hugs Dustin again. Dustin struggles to get away,
but Jack won't let him. Dustin finally breaks down in
uncontrollable tears.

                    DUSTIN
          Then I'm going to make his
          invention happen!

                    JACK
          That, I would like to see.

Ward smiles at Jack.

                    DUSTIN
          Erin is smart as hell about this
          stuff.

                    JACK
          She and Ling will be a good start.

INT. OFFICE - TRANSAMERICA BUILDING

In the adjacent office, a YOUNG MAN who has obviously been
eavesdropping and taping their conversation takes off his
headphones, and scurries out of the office.

INT. OFFICE HALLWAY

The young man inconspicuously enters the elevator with Jack and Dustin.

INT. OFFICE

12 MEN (50's) ring a large expensive oval conference table. Roman stands nervously at the head of the table facing the ominous group. Only the BACKS OF THEIR HEADS are visible.

                    MAN #1
          What do you have to report?

                    ROMAN
          The boy is in possession of
          advanced blueprints and equat--

                    MAN #1
          WILL he develop them?

                    ROMAN
          At this point, we have no reason to
          believe so, sir.

The man looks around the group, assuming they will agree with his stance.

                    MAN #1
          Pay him off or get rid of him.

                    ROMAN
          Yes sir.

EXT. HELICOPTER PAD

Jack and Dustin exit the copter and get back in Jack's truck.

INT. TRUCK

Jack and Dustin drive down the gravel road.

                    RADIO
          ...unemployment Levels are reaching
          20%, consumer confidence levels at
          all time lows--

                    JACK
          Don't be so greedy, 5 mill is
          enough.

                    DUSTIN
          I know, I know, but jeez. How much
          did he give away again?

INT. JACK'S LODGE

Jack and Dustin put their bags down. Ling hugs Jack.

                    LING SUN
          Dustin, I made your favorite beef
          bourgoinine.

                    DUSTIN
          No thanks. Good night.

Dustin gives a listless wave. Jack nods to Ling that he'll
explain everything.

INT. BEDROOM - JACK'S LODGE

Dustin talks on the phone.

                    REBECCA (ON TELEPHONE)
          That money was yours. That's a
          disgusting amount to give to
          charity.

                    DUSTIN
          Yeah, I know.

A GRUNT echoes from the background over the phone.

                    REBECCA
          Well, I've got to get back to my
          work.

                    DUSTIN
          I'll be back next week.

The phone CLICKS. Dustin holds out the phone, annoyed at her
rudeness.

INT. REBECCA'S HIDEAWAY

Rebecca stands in a leather teddy, WHIP in hand, in a cement
floored room. Various RESTRAINT EQUIPMENT sits in the room.
A computer SCREEN shows MISTRESS R. Rebecca types in a few
strokes and pushes ENTER with her free hand. She CRACKS the
whip on a chubby GIMP (20) wearing a leather mask with a red
ball GAG in his mouth, a la "Pulp Fiction". His wispy dirty
blond hair struggles to get out of the leather mask.

                    GIMP
                 (muffled)
OWWWWWWWWW!

He fidgets.

                    REBECCA
          Never make a sound while I'm on the
          phone.

She whips him again.

                    REBECCA (cont'd)
          5 measly million, uggh.

He GRUNTS more. She undoes his red ball GAG.

                    GIMP
          Mistress Rebecca, will you please
          get me out of this.

                    REBECCA
          I'm not done with you yet.

She cracks the whip on him again.

                    GIMP

          I...I've got to take a shit.

                    REBECCA
          Oh, you are so disgusting. That is
          SO going to cost you extra.

                    GIMP
          OK, but just hurry.

Rebecca undoes his restraints. He scurries in to the
bathroom.

                    GIMP (O.S.) (cont'd)
          Ohhhhh.

The familiar PLOP of a turd hitting the water makes Rebecca's
face wince.

Rebecca fans the air in front of her face.

                    REBECCA
          Ohhh my God. TRIPLE!

                    GIMP (O.S.)
                 (whining)
          I'm sorry.

He comes out of the bathroom. We see him as the chubby dork
next door, but in leather bikini underwear looking remarkably
like Jack Osborne, of Osborne TV family fame.

                    REBECCA
          I've got another client coming over
          here in 20 minutes. He's going to
          think I did that!

Rebecca continues to wave her hand in front of her face.

                    GIMP
          Can I bust a nut before I leave?

The gimp plunges his hand into his bikini.

                    REBECCA
          Absolutely not. You gave up that
          chance.

                    GIMP
          It was the damn chili.

                    REBECCA
          Save it.

The Gimp puts his clothes on.

                    GIMP
          Can we do that rape scene thing I
          wanna try next ti--

                    REBECCA
          You are so NOT going to touch me
          with your little corkscrew.

                    GIMP
             (earnestly)
          I've been using the penis pump you
          sold me. It's not that little
          anymore. I wouldn't really hit you
          or anything.

Rebecca gets an idea.

                    REBECCA
          But...I do know someone.

Rebecca shows the Gimp a picture of Dustin and Erin together.

                    GIMP
          Wow! She's hot.

                         REBECCA
          She's not that hot.

                         GIMP
             Is she in to it?

An evil grin overtakes her face.

                         GIMP (cont'd)
          Does she work with you?

Rebecca straightens the Gimp's hair to show him affection.

INT. DINING ROOM - JACK'S LODGE - EVENING

Dustin and Erin enter from a hike. Erin carries a roll of
BLUEPRINTS.

                         LING SUN
             Dinner is served.

Everyone sits and admires the exquisitely set candle lit
dining table. Each place has 12 pieces of silver and 3
various sized expensive Baccarat glasses. Erin puts the
blueprint roll behind her.

                         ERIN
             I've got to show professor
             Hartwell. He's a major brain and
             totally in to this stuff.

                         DUSTIN
          No. You can't show anyone.

                         ERIN
             Dustin, sure I'm smart, but there's
             no way. You can trust him. He
             teaches a whole class on
             alternative energy.

Dustin looks at Jack for approval. Jack nods, it's
necessary.

                         LING SUN
             Smart guy. I've footnoted him many
             times.

                         JACK
          But just him.

                         LING SUN
             A toast.

Ling raises her crystal wine glass.

                    LING SUN (cont'd)
          To a better world.

The group clinks and beams.

INT. OFFICE - BERKELEY - DAY

Dustin, Jack, Ling and Erin ring around PROFESSOR HARTWELL
(50), dressed like a modern hippie in round glasses and
Birkenstocks.

                    ERIN
          Why haven't we figured this out
          before?

                    PROFESSOR HARTWELL
          There's scientists all over the
          world bouncing around the answers
          proven here. Like the Stellarator
          project.

Hartwell points to various proof equations on the plan, Ling
observes and nods.

                    PROFESSOR HARTWELL (cont'd)
          But they said Alternating Current
          wouldn't work either and gave the
          same excuses. Who knows, maybe
          even Tesla wasn't the first.

                    ERIN
          Can we do it?

                    PROFESSOR HARTWELL
          Anything you can imagine will
          become a reality, sooner or later.

Erin hugs Dustin.

                    PROFESSOR HARTWELL (cont'd)
          It's going to take time...and
          money. Lots of money.

                    DUSTIN
          We've got both.

They look with excitement into each others eyes. The
electricity of verging on something great is unstoppable.

INT. DORM HALLWAY - AFTERNOON

Erin stands with a loaded bookbag at Dustin's door, talking
excitedly.

Rebecca slithers up, annoyed at Erin.

                    ERIN
          Oh, Hi Rebecca.

Rebecca scans her from head to toe in disgust.

                    REBECCA
          Hi.

                    ERIN
          Talk to you tomorrow Dust.

                    DUSTIN
          You got it.

Rebecca slams the door behind her.

INT. DORM ROOM

                    REBECCA
          You said--

Dustin exhales.

                    DUSTIN
          Relax. I told you. We're good
          friends.

                    REBECCA
          Because momma's not gonna put out
          if she's not number one, and the
          only one.

Rebecca slaps Dustin on the butt. Dustin smiles.

She pulls her sweater off revealing a sexy bra. She slips
her pants off and then fumbles with his pants button.

                    DUSTIN
          Nice bra.

                    REBECCA
          They were having a sale at Macy's,
          but I couldn't afford the bottoms.
          You should have seen them.

                    DUSTIN
          Definitely have to go get those.

Rebecca starts to kiss his chest. He takes a wad of BILLS
off his desk and tosses them on her clothes. Her mood
changes to high gear as she tugs his underwear off to reveal
his nice butt. His head cocks back.

INT. LIVING ROOM - JACK'S LODGE - EVENING

Jack rests his legs over Ling's lap on the couch.

                    LING SUN
          Erin is SO much better than Rebecca
          for Dustin.

                    JACK
          Oh, Rebecca's all right.

                    LING SUN
               (singing)
          "Gold digging girls, got me crazy I
          can't take it no more.

                    JACK
          Guess it takes one to know one.

Jack smirks and kisses her.

                    LING SUN
               (Asian hooker)
          But who make-a yo egg ro' squirt?

Jack nods like a little boy and gives her a more passionate
kiss.

                    LING SUN (cont'd)
               (normal voice)
          We haven't heard much from the
          "creepers" lately.

                    JACK
          They followed Dust and I yesterday.

                    LING SUN
          Really?

                    JACK
          You're right though, they've been
          pretty quiet.

                         LING SUN
          Except for the Satellite dish guy
          for that upgrade it's been a ghost
          town.

                         JACK
          What upgrade?

Jack jerks up from the couch.

                         JACK (cont'd)
          Goddamnit Ling! You know you have
          to tell me everything.

                         LING SUN
          I..I was right there watching.

Jack jumps to a kitchen drawer revealing a strange electrical
wand, similar to a metal detector at airport security. He
turns it on. It BEEPS frantically.

Jack moves the wand over the living room. He walks towards
the window and the curtains. The lights move wildly and
there are intermittent loud BEEPS.

                         JACK
          Apparently not the whole...time.

Jack pulls a chair over to the CURTAIN ROD and stands on it.

He holds the wand toward the end of the rod. The light fully
illuminates.

Jack pulls out a CAMERA smaller than the tip of his pinkie
and examines it.

INT. CONTROL ROOM

Greeley and Raquel rip their headsets off to avoid the
squealing FEEDBACK.

                         GREELEY
          We still have the other one in the
          bedroom.

On the SCREEN, a CLOSE UP of Jack's face appears, and then
his feet. The picture goes black, and then appears baby
blue, staring at a hazy light in the distance.

EXT. DECK

Jack looks down over his lit pool. He returns inside.

INT. CONTROL ROOM

Greeley admires the screen.

                    GREELEY
          Cool, I didn't know they were
          waterproof.

The screen shows a beautiful BLUE, but then goes to SNOW.

                    RAQUEL
          They're not.

INT. LIVING ROOM

Jack re-enters the room. Ling knows she screwed up.

                    JACK
          No one can EVER!...ever come here
          without my knowledge.

                    LING SUN
          I know. I'm sorry. I wanted to
          save you time. You've been with
          Dustin working so much, I didn't
          wan--

                    JACK
          Promise me.

                    LING SUN
          I promise.

Jack softens.

                    JACK
          OK.

                    LING SUN
          Jeanine called and was feeling
          pretty low so I invited her up
          tomorrow.

                    JACK
          That was nice.

Jack hugs Ling.

INT. CONTROL ROOM

ROMAN (50) dressed in a custom dark suit, hurries in to the
room.

                    ROMAN
          Snow on the mountains.

                    GREELEY
          I know sir.

                    ROMAN
          Get 49 in there again. Damnit!

Roman walks to the other side of the room where other young
people scan hundreds of surveillance screens.

Roman continues down the row of desks.

He stops at BARRY's desk, (24)ultra clean cut, and pale.

                    ROMAN (cont'd)
          What's going on in the Oval Office?

                    BARRY
          The president vetoed all detractory
          legislation for our interests sir.

Another YOUNG MAN scurries in to the room, hands Roman a
REPORT and exits.

                    YOUNG MAN #2
          Cameras are off on Energy 8 sir.

                    ROMAN
          I know...I know.

Roman rubs his face and continues to Greeley.

                    ROMAN (cont'd)
          Greeley, this is your project, keep
          an eye on him and those tramps he's
          been running with. Is she one of
          ours?

Barry vies to be Roman's pet and is jealous of Greeley.

                    GREELEY
          No sir.

                    ROMAN
          Find out more of who she is. Maybe
          we can use her.

                    GREELEY
          Already have sir. Rebecca Watson.
          She has a sex business on the side
          to pay for her schooling.
                    (MORE)

                         GREELEY (cont'd)
                    Religious parents in Modesto,
                    oldest of 2 children.

                         ROMAN
                    Good, something we can use against
                    her.

                         GREELEY
                    49 has been contacted. She has
                    promised new devices by tomorrow.

                         ROMAN
                    Sooner! Use XV97's, they're
                    undetectable. He's getting too
                    good.

                         GREELEY
                    Already delivered to her, sir.

                         ROMAN
                    Let's get a money proposal to
                    Dustin.

Roman pats Greeley's shoulder and continues out of the room.
Greeley's face shows obvious disdain for Roman.

INT. DORM HALLWAY

A man in a suit presents a PACKAGE to Dustin. Dustin looks
at it and hands it back quickly. The man pushes it back to
Dustin.

                         DUSTIN
                    How much?

The man quiets flabbergasted Dustin, hands him his CARD and
walks away.

INT. DORM ROOM

Dustin enters leafing through the package. Rebecca waits for
him on the bed.

                         REBECCA
                    Who was that guy?

                         DUSTIN
                    Some guy who wants to pay me a lot
                    of money.

                         REBECCA
                    How much?

                         DUSTIN
               100 million.

Rebecca jumps up in glee.

                         REBECCA
               Baby, that awesome!

She hugs Dustin.

                         REBECCA (cont'd)
               I'm so happy for us/you.

                         DUSTIN
               Yeah, we'll see. I've got to talk
               to Jack about it.

Rebecca seems annoyed the deal isn't sealed, and rubs his
shoulders.

INT. DINING ROOM - JACK'S LODGE

Jeanine, Line, Jack and Dustin dine on a gourmet meal of
trout.

Dustin barely eats.

                         JEANINE
               How's school?

Dustin just stares at her and doesn't answer.

                         JACK
               You...in the conference room.

Dustin looks defiant.

                         JACK (cont'd)
               Now!

Dustin mopes toward the office, a bunch of ROLLED PAPERS
stick out of his rear jean's pocket.

Dustin sprawls insolently in Jack's office chair while jack
sits on the desk facing him.

                         JACK (cont'd)
               She's hurting too. Aren't you
               human?

Dustin gets up to leave.

                         DUSTIN
               Get her a dog or a vibrator. She
               can afford one.

Jack slams him back in his seat.

                         JACK
               For your information buster, she
               gave most of her portion to
               charity.

                         DUSTIN
               Well good. Then I won't feel so
               bad about doing this.

Dustin grabs the DOCUMENTS from his back pocket and slaps
them on the desk. Jack delves in to the information.

                         JACK
               You've got to be fucking kidding
               me.

                         DUSTIN
               No, I'm not. You've got an easy
               life. Why can't I have one?

                         JACK
               Because you have a chance to better
               the world. Do you think I'm proud
               of hiding from life?

                         DUSTIN
               They said they'd develop it.

                         JACK
               And you believe them?

                         DUSTIN
               Look man. It's not my job to
               change the world. I can be a good
               person surfing on my private
               island.

                         JACK
               I won't let you do it.

Dustin gets up, Jack restrains him.

                         DUSTIN
               Great, you gonna smack me around
               like your first wife?

Jack looks like he might take a swing. Jack relents.

                         JACK
             You're as stubborn as your father.

Dustin starts to cry.

                         DUSTIN
             And you're not him.

Dustin jerks away from him and runs out of the room. He runs
out the front door. Jack slowly walks out of his office.
Ling starts after Dustin.

                         JACK
             Let him go.

INT. DORM ROOM - LATE NIGHT

Dustin walks in with Rebecca. She comforts him.

They lie down the bed. Dustin looks at the ceiling.

                         REBECCA
             How come you never take me
             anywhere?

                         DUSTIN
             Whadya mean? We just went to that
             fancy place at the top of--

                         REBECCA
             I mean around your friends.

                         DUSTIN
             I dunno.

Rebecca plays with his chest and stares in his eyes.

                         DUSTIN (cont'd)
             What?

                         REBECCA
             Take me to the Cal/Stanford game.

                         DUSTIN
             It's kind of a buddy thing.

                         REBECCA
             We can all go together.

Dustin goes for a kiss. She holds him to stop.

                         DUSTIN
             Alright.

She allows him to kiss her.

INT. DORM HALLWAY - NIGHT

Dustin creeps out of his dorm room in his boxers looking
freshly sexed. Fred, his friend from the funeral, approaches
him from behind.

                    FRED
          Who you got in there this time?

                    DUSTIN
          Nobody man. I gotta pee.

Dustin is on his tip toes ready to pee his boxers.

                    FRED
          Nobody huh, how bout I just go in
          there and give nobody a go.

Fred rubs his hands together and jokingly starts to unbuckle
his jeans.

                    DUSTIN
          Rebecca.

Fred recoils.

                    FRED
          Dude, she is nasty. I heard she
          bones for cash.

                    DUSTIN
          Nah dude, she's cool.

                    FRED
          I'm not dipping my golden wick in
          your stank anyhoo.

                    DUSTIN
          Hah.

                    FRED
          We've got a huge spodey for the
          game tomorrow.

                    DUSTIN
          It's cool if I bring Rebecca,
          right.

                    FRED
          Man, you always pull this. Bros
          before hos, literally in this case.

> DUSTIN
> It's all good dude.

Dustin gives him the SECRET HANDSHAKE.

Fred makes a "L" sign on his forehead.

> FRED
> Man, you used to be fun.

> DUSTIN
> Dude, I can still out smoke, drink
> and surf you.

> FRED
> Please nigguh.

> DUSTIN
> How come you can say "Nigger" and I
> can't.

> FRED
> Because you put an E-R on the end.

> DUSTIN
> That's so fucked up. Tomorrow.

The SPECIAL HANDSHAKE ensues once more.

Dustin darts down the hall.

Rebecca pokes her head out of his door to see what's the commotion. Fred walks towards his room past her.

> FRED
> Hey Rebecca.

Rebecca looks at him and completely snubs him.

Fred keys in to his room.

> FRED (cont'd)
>   (to himself)
> That bitch must have some crazy
> kind of pussy.

INT. REBECCA'S HIDEAWAY - DAY

The gimp slurps from a BIG GULP cup. She points to a MAP of UC BERKELEY. Several pictures of Erin sit on the edge of her desk.

                  REBECCA
         It's got to be a little dark.

Rebecca presents him a plaster arm CAST and sling.

                  REBECCA (cont'd)
         So you put this on and then you ask
         her to help you with your books to
         your car.

                  GIMP
         That's genius!

Rebecca gives him a rarely seen smile.

                  REBECCA
         Isn't it. I got that from a
         Discovery channel show on Ted
         Bundy.

                  GIMP
         But I'm not gonna really hurt her,
         right?

                  REBECCA
         I told you we had girl talk, and
         she's always had this fantasy.

                  GIMP
         Why can't we just invite her ov--

                  REBECCA
         Look, do you want to live your
         fantasy or not?

The Gimp looks at pictures of Erin and then down at his
tented pants.

                  GIMP
         Yeah, I like it. She looks kind of
         innocent though, not like you.

Rebecca jumps up and puts him in a half nelson.

                  GIMP (cont'd)
         Ow! Rebecca, my glasses are hurti--

                  REBECCA
         It's Mistress to you, now try to
         get out of this.

The gimp struggles a bit.

                    GIMP
          Wow, that's really good. Ow!

                    REBECCA
          Are you a man or a pussy?

                    GIMP
          I'm no pussy.

Rebecca pulls his head over to the MAP of campus.

                    REBECCA
          She gets out of Physics at 6. You
          wait here.

Rebecca points to the map. The gimp nods, still in the half
nelson. She cranks it harder.

                    REBECCA (cont'd)
          Like this.

EXT. UC BERKELEY CAMPUS

The campus CLOCKTOWER reads 6:04. Erin waves goodbye to her
friends, including Fred. She carries her backpack and a
stack of papers in the other.

                    FRED
          See you at the game.

The gimp lurks near a tree with his arm in the cast and
sling. His free arm is overloaded with a large stack of
books.

The gimp starts in front of her and drops all of his books.
He looks around flustered. Erin rushes to his rescue.

                    ERIN
          Here let me help you with that.

The gimp is awed by her beauty. He wants to just kiss her,
not rape her.

                    GIMP
          My car is right over here.

Erin walks to the passenger door.

                    GIMP (cont'd)
          That side is broken. Would you
          mind putting them inside?

                    ERIN
          Sure.

The gimp follows her to the driver side and keys open the
door.

>   GIMP
>   Just put them in there.

Erin struggles to get the large stack of books on the
passenger seat. She climbs in more. The gimp awkwardly
pushes her in all the way. She's startled.

He quickly hops in and puts the keys in the ignition and revs
the engine.

>   ERIN
>   What are you doing?

>   GIMP
>   Uh, thought I would give you a ride
>   to where you are going--

The gimp pushes the auto lock. Erin is alarmed.

>   ERIN
>   No, let me out!

The gimp needs to act fast.

>   ERIN (cont'd)
>   Now!

He panics and puts her in a crude half nelson just as Rebecca
taught him.

>   ERIN (cont'd)
>   What are you doing?

Erin punches him wildly. She grabs his crotch with full
force and twists.

>   GIMP
>   Owwww! Ummm...That's really good.

He lets her out of the headlock to attend to his painful
crotch. She takes her huge Physics book and jabs the corner
of it full force into his eye.

>   GIMP (cont'd)
>   Urggghhh! That's hot.

Erin hits the door lock, it pops open.

She goes to get out of the gimp's side. He is terrified, but
loving it. She is baffled.

                        ERIN
           My side's broken.

                        GIMP
           No it's not.

Erin smacks him over the head with another book, grabs her
things from the floor accidently including his "DUNGEONS AND
DRAGONS SECRETS" book and jumps out.

                        ERIN
           Creep!

The gimp SQUEALS the tires and races away.

INT. PROFESSOR HARTWELL'S OFFICE

Dustin hugs Erin who is more mad than scared now. Dustin
examines the book from the car.

                        DUSTIN
           He's probably a harmless geek that
           got a little excited.

Dustin discovers a CARD. It reads: Mistress R, Domination
and House Cleaning. He doesn't let Erin see it, and shoves
it back in the book.

                        ERIN
           Was this the guys you were talking
           about?

                  PROFESSOR HARTWELL
           If THEY would have wanted you, THEY
           would have gotten you.

Dustin looks concerned.

                PROFESSOR HARTWELL (cont'd)
           I'm going to need you both full
           time next week. Are you with me?

Dustin goes to grab his PAPERS from his rear pocket and
almost blurts out their offer, but stops.

                PROFESSOR HARTWELL (cont'd)
           Were you going to say something
           Dustin?

Dustin says nothing.

INT. CONTROL ROOM

Greeley rests his hand on his chin daydreaming to the monitor
at a CLOSE UP of Erin inside the professor's office. Roman
approaches with a serious face.

                    ROMAN
          Whitaker says the Tesla plan may be
          in motion. You said--

Roman notices the close up of Erin on the monitor.

                    ROMAN (cont'd)
          I knew you weren't ready for this
          responsibility!

Roman angrily pushes several buttons and clicks through
several monitors of familiar places. The monitors show: the
NATIONAL MONUMENT, the OVAL OFFICE, the interior of the
UNITED NATIONS BUILDING, specifically at the IRAQ and SAUDI
ARABIA seats and finally back to Erin and Hartwell.

                    ROMAN (cont'd)
          What's their next move?

                    GREELEY
          I think they may abandon the
          project sir.

Roman observes the screen.

                    GREELEY (cont'd)
          Sir, I believe they've hit a snag
          in the plans.

                    ROMAN
          Maybe we won't have to take the lot
          of them out.

Greeley is relieved Roman believed his lie. Greeley analyzes
the TV MONITOR watching the heated conversation of Dustin and
Professor Hartwell. Dustin holds the DOCUMENTS.

                    ROMAN (cont'd)
          Turn it up. I want to hear this.

Greeley must act fast. Instead of pulling the plug on his
earphones, he pulls the plug on everything sending the
screens to BLACK.

                    ROMAN (cont'd)
          Greeley. Have you been smoking
          marijuana again?

Roman angrily grabs his face and looks in his eyes.

>   GREELEY
>   No sir.

He brusquely releases his face.

>   ROMAN
>   Apples don't fall too far from the
>   tree. But my charitable heart--

Greeley quickly goes to repair his purposeful outage. The
monitors kick back on. Roman grabs Greeley's headphones.
Greeley makes them squeal with FEEDBACK. Roman drops the
headphones in disgust.

>   GREELEY
>   Sorry sir.

Greeley notices the three beginning to disperse. He finally
connects the sound.

ON MONITOR:

>   DUSTIN
>   You're right.

Dustin hugs the professor and leaves with Erin.

The professor stays in the room, looking very concerned,
staring at the plans.

>   GREELEY
>   He looks baffled sir.

>   ROMAN
>   Stay on them.

>   GREELEY
>   You know it's my project sir.

Greeley sneers at Roman walking away. Roman looks back at
Greeley who then switches to a pleasant face.

EXT. QUADRANGLE

Dustin walks with Fred. Fred holds the "MISTRESS R CARD".

>   FRED
>   Detective Fred is gonna figure this
>   shit out.

                    DUSTIN
          All right man.

They do the secret handshake.

                    FRED
          Tomorrow.

EXT. UC BERKELEY STADIUM - BLEACHERS - DAY

The packed stadium brims with people dressed in blue and
gold.

Dustin's rowdy friends, including Fred and Erin, revel in the
time of their lives, drinking their special BOOTLEG and
laughing at next to nothing.

10 rows up, Dustin sits hunched over next to Rebecca, bored
out of his mind, looking at the rowdy bunch having fun. Fred
turns toward Dustin while Rebecca looks away and taunts him,
mouthing the word "bitch". Dustin flips him the bird.
Rebecca notices.

                    REBECCA
          Don't be immature like them. We
          all have to grow up sometime.

                    DUSTIN
          I like being immature.

Dustin crosses his arms like a pouting boy. He looks
longingly down at Fred and the gang. Erin walks up to the
group with a pile of junk food and disappears into their mob.

Rebecca is really annoyed now.

                    REBECCA
          Let's take a walk.

                    DUSTIN
          Where?

                    REBECCA
          Anywhere.

Dustin trudges behind Rebecca up the stairs to the landing
above the seats.

EXT. LANDING ABOVE BLEACHERS

Food and drink CONCESSIONS line the wide walkway.
Expressionless, Dustin and Rebecca walk arm in arm past the
stands. A young man in sunglasses, dressed in blue and gold
like a Cal Bear's fan, walks toward Dustin and jockeys in his
way, friendly nodding "excuse me". It's Greeley.

                    REBECCA
          There's Shawn.

Rebecca and Dustin walk over to SHAWN(19) and two friends,
all dressed in solid black. Each of their manes are dyed a
wine color. Their fingernails even match as they desperately
hold on to the Goth era of the early 90's.

                    REBECCA (cont'd)
                (affected sophistication)
          Hello Ladies.

                    SHAWN
          Hello Rebecca.

Shawn ignores Dustin and even turns her back to him.

                    DUSTIN
          I'll be right over here.

Dustin points and walks toward a concession stand.

Rebecca nods.

                    DUSTIN (cont'd)
          You girls wanna dog?

                    REBECCA
          Ewww, they are so--

Dustin shrugs and turns away.

Rebecca delves in to evil gossip conversation with Shawn and
company.

Dustin walks over to the concession stand. A ROAR from the
crowd beckons Dustin to the edge of the stadium. He peers
down the bleachers to look down at Fred and the gang. Fred
and Erin high five and hug each other. A chubby smiling GIRL
refills both their eager glasses with spodey.

Dustin spins around to Rebecca, but he can't resist his pals.
He scampers down the stairs to Fred, wolfing down his hot dog
in two bites. He bear hugs Fred from behind who still chews
his food.

Greeley looks down from the top of the stairs, longing to be part of their camaraderie.

EXT. UC BERKELEY - BLEACHERS

                    FRED
          Who else has the strength of ten
          men.

Fred turns around to hug Dustin.

                    FRED (cont'd)
          Where's Cruella?

                    DUSTIN
          Up there with the chicks in the
          black lipstick.

                    ERIN
          Such not the good look.

Erin gives Dustin a hug, and a quick but soft kiss on the lips. Now that she has a buzz, she can't hide her true feelings.

                    ERIN (cont'd)
          Hey bud.

They kiss one more time. Their mutual attraction scares them both. They release.

                    ERIN (cont'd)
               (whispering to Dustin)
          Prof is making big progress.

                    DUSTIN
          Cool.

Rebecca looks down from the top of the stands at Dustin rapt in conversation with Erin. She storms down to Dustin.

                    REBECCA
          Dustin, honey, where's my hot dog?

Fred starts laughing.

                    FRED
          I thought he gave you that this
          morning?

Dustin laughs. Erin smirks at the ground. Rebecca forces Dustin's smile away.

> DUSTIN
> You said you didn't want one.

> REBECCA
> I changed my mind.

Dustin rolls his eyes to Fred and Erin.

> ERIN
> You guys come back, OK?

> REBECCA
> I don't think so.

Rebecca scoops Dustin and turns him around pushing him up the stairs.

Greeley observes the whole interaction.

Dustin looks around one more time at his pals. He is pissed.

> DUSTIN
> Now you know why I don't bring you
> out with them.

> REBECCA
> What?

> DUSTIN
> You made me feel like shit.

> REBECCA
> You're not like them.

> DUSTIN
> Nobody is like anybody if you don't
> talk to them.

> REBECCA
> Don't get so mad.

Rebecca comforts Dustin.

EXT. LANDING ABOVE BLEACHERS

Rebecca pulls him close to her and kisses him sweetly. One hand descends to his crotch.

> REBECCA
> Let's go back to your place.

She bites his ear.

                        DUSTIN
              It's almost the last game of the
              season.

Dustin looks toward the ROAR.

She pulls him closer. Dustin begins to forget her
bitchiness. The Goth girls approach, cancelling Rebecca
allure and Dustin's chubby-in-progress.

                        SHAWN
              Rebecca?

                        DUSTIN
              Actually, why don't you hang with
              them, and we'll hook up later.

Dustin stares at her with a blank face. Rebecca wants to
appear in complete control in front of the Goth girls and
chooses not to fight.

                        DUSTIN (cont'd)
              Ladies.

Dustin waves at them all, spins around and heads into the
bleachers.

                        REBECCA
              Dustin. Meet me in your room
              later.

Rebecca stares at him to try her manipulative power.

                        DUSTIN
              Deal. See you rockers later.

Dustin mocks them in an endearing way, shaking his head a la
Heavy Metal band headbanger and shooting them a "hang loose"
sign.

Dustin runs down the stairs to the gang.

EXT. UC BERKELEY - BLEACHERS

                        FRED
              I knew you'd be back.

Fred gives him another hug. Erin's eyes light up, she
squeezes his arm.

                        ERIN
              Hey!

Dustin and Erin look in to each others eyes knowing they are the ones for each other.

INT. DORM HALLWAY - EVENING

Dustin is buzzed. He approaches his door and notices it's cracked open. He hears Rebecca on her cell phone and peers through the door with a horny grin. She lies in her bra and panties gazing at DOCUMENTS on the bed.

                    REBECCA
          Don't you worry sir. I've got him
          wrapped around my finger.

Rebecca notices someone peering through the door.

                    REBECCA (cont'd)
               (whispering in phone)
          He's here.

She closes her phone and spins around seductively.

                    REBECCA (cont'd)
          What took you so long sweetums.

                    DUSTIN
          So what's your cut.

                    REBECCA
          I,uh..just--

Dustin becomes enraged.

                    DUSTIN
          How much!

                    REBECCA
          Like 5%, like a broker. Relax
          baby.

                    DUSTIN
          It's gonna be 5% of nothing.

Dustin grabs his backpack off the desk and spins around.

                    REBECCA
               (sweetly)
          Dustin?

She realizes he's finished with her.

>   REBECCA (cont'd)
>   (screaming)
>   Dustin!

He grabs some loose change off his desk, holds it up to her like she might steal it and starts to exit.

>   REBECCA (cont'd)
>   (sweet again)
>   Dustin.

He heads out the door.

>   REBECCA (cont'd)
>   He said you're not supposed to
>   leave.

SLAM. Dustin wants to turn around and give her a piece of his mind, but hesitates. Just then Fred comes out of his room waving a PRINTOUT.

>   FRED
>   Dude! I was right.

He runs up to Dustin to show him the PICTURE of Rebecca dressed in a leather teddy holding a whip.

KABOOOM! A powerful explosion blasts the door off Dustin's room thrusting Fred on top of Dustin. Dustin is covered in debris and shakes his head to breathe. 2 SHARP METAL SHARDS stick out of Fred's back. Dustin notices the shards.

>   DUSTIN
>   Dude, it's gonna be all right.
>   Don't move.

Fred can barely speak, and GASPS for air.

>   FRED
>   Man, I was right. GASP. I was
>   right.

Fred starts to drift and gurgle blood. Dustin weeps.

>   DUSTIN
>   Don't die, you fucker.

Dustin hugs him.

>   DUSTIN (cont'd)
>   I need you man.

>   FRED
>   You're my nigguh.

Fred softly pats Dustin to keep him from crying. He attempts
to give him their secret handshake, but he's losing
consciousness.

                    DUSTIN
          Come on man.

Dustin hugs him tighter and cries. Fred expires, eyes open.

2 men in suits spot Dustin and point. Dustin struggles from
under Fred and darts down the hall. SHOTS are fired. He
runs up the fire escape stairs.

EXT. TREE

Dustin climbs out the window and hides in the dense foliage.

Dustin watches the man run up the stairs and then down. Two
men stand underneath the tree, look around and scatter. The
fire engines begin to arrive. Dustin tries to get back in
the window. It' won't open. He hangs from a branch and
jumps, running in to the dark.

INT. ERIN'S DORM ROOM

Erin studies lying on her bed. Dustin sneaks in, flips off
the light and covers Erin's mouth. Erin is pleased.

                    ERIN
          Hey.

                    DUSTIN
          Shhh.

Dustin goes to the window.

                    ERIN
          Oh my God, you're bleeding. What--

                    DUSTIN
          We've got to get out of here.

                    ERIN
          Wha, why? Are you still drunk?

Dustin looks out the window from the darkened room. He sees
the 2 MEN from the dorm approaching Greeley. He strains to
hear what they're saying.

EXT. GIRL'S DORM

Greeley speaks with the two men. The SIRENS consume the
background noise.

>   GREELEY
>   Her room is clear. Why wasn't I
>   involved?

>   MAN #1
>   We had our orders.

The men hurry away. Greeley looks back at Erin's darkened
room window.

INT. ERIN'S DORM ROOM

>   ERIN
>   Who are they?

Dustin hugs Erin and starts to cry.

>   DUSTIN
>   I'm so scared. I'm so sorry I got
>   you in this.

Erin comforts him.

>   DUSTIN (cont'd)
>   Fred.

>   ERIN
>   Let's get Fred.

>   DUSTIN
>   He's, he's dead.

Dustin weeps stronger. Dustin's cell phone RINGS. JACK
appears on the caller id.

>   DUSTIN (cont'd)
>   Jack, I'm sorry. You were right.

>   JACK (O.S.)
>   Meet me at the place where you
>   thought you could do anything.

>   DUSTIN
>   What? Where?

>   JACK
>   Destroy your phone.

                         DUSTIN
          What?

                         JACK
          And make sure you're alone.

                         DUSTIN
          Stop. I don't underst--

                         JACK
          I'll bring the worms

Dustin phone clicks silent. He looks baffled at Erin.

                         DUSTIN
          Fuck.

Dustin is frustrated but then gets a clue and nods.

EXT. BOAT DOCK - AFTERNOON

Dustin parks his beat a beat-up Dodge Colt in a dirt parking
lot. A boat dock seen from the picture as a youth floats on
the lake. Dustin and Erin exit the car.

                         DUSTIN
          Nobody should have drive a car like
          that.

Dustin slams the door. It pops back open. He slams it again,
and pushes it shut with his hip.

                         ERIN
          I'll be sure and let my brother
          know how appreciative you are.

Dustin walks out on the rickety dock and slaps his thigh in
exasperation.

                         DUSTIN
          Where else would he have fucking
          meant.

CRACKLE, CRACK, twigs break. Erin jumps to Dustin. They
look toward the noise.

                         ERIN
          Oh my God! You scared me.

Jack appears walking out of the woods. Dustin and he
immediately hug.

                    DUSTIN
          Sorry Jack.

                    JACK
          I'm sorry too. I heard about
          Rebecca and Fred.

Dustin nods and hugs him tighter.

                    DUSTIN
          Where's the professor?

                    JACK
          He was with me?

Dustin is puzzled. He looks at Erin, she just smiles that
she knows something else.

Jack motions them to walk along a path through the trees.

INT. FOREST

The group stops at a mighty REDWOOD TREE. Jack moves a
branch and a section of the tree trunk opens as a DOOR. Jack
motions the amazed group inside. They walk down wooden
stairs.

INT. TREE TRUNK LABORATORY

Professor Hartwell and Ling wear dark safety goggles and work
diligently, welding their project. Ling catches their eye
and nods to the professor who stops and removes his goggles,
looking apologetic to Dustin.

                    PROFESSOR HARTWELL
          I feel a little dishonest.

                    LING SUN
          We've been working together for 10
          years.

                    JACK
          Dustin, I needed to know you were
          truly on board before I told you.

Dustin looks down at the ground.

                    DUSTIN
          I don't blame you. Did you know?

Dustin looks at Erin. Erin nods her head sheepishly.

                    ERIN
          But I thought you were cute before
          they told me who you were.

                    PROFESSOR HARTWELL
          We've got one more month until the
          show.

Professor shows Dustin a FLYER, it reads: WORLD ENERGY
SYMPOSIUM, MOSCONE CENTER, SAN FRANCISCO.

                    LING SUN
          We need your help.

                    DUSTIN
          Don't you know what just happened?

Dustin slaps down his hands in exasperation and shakes his
head.

                    DUSTIN (cont'd)
          They'll kill all of us.

INT. CONFERENCE ROOM

Roman again stands in front of the ominous group seated at
the large conference table. By the look on his face, he has
just gotten his ass chewed.

                    ROMAN
          But sir, it wasn't my fault.

                    MAN #1
          How can a 19 year old boy just
          disappear?

                    ROMAN
          I, uh..uh--

                    MAN #1
          And what about his uncle?

                    ROMAN
          We have them fully surveilled, and
          another camera going in tonight.

                    MAN #1
          Once they release the proof of the
          physics on this technology. No one
          can stop it.

INT. TREE TRUNK LABORATORY

The group works diligently on the prototype. Dustin sits
nearby and studies manuals.

                    DUSTIN
          Trip out. It's the same chemical
          reaction as the sun.

                    JACK
          Turn that light bulb off above your
          head and help us lift this.

Dustin puts down the manual and hops over to assist.

                    JACK (cont'd)
          And up!

The group lifts the 4 X 4 PROTOTYPE over to a sturdy table.

NOTE TO READER: THE "STELLARATOR" AND THE "TOKAMAK" ARE
ACTUAL DEVICES IN DEVELOPMENT FOR OVER 50 YEARS THAT BOTH
UTILIZE MAGNETIC FUSION ENERGY. THEY BOTH BEND PLASMA INTO
TOROIDAL SHAPES SUSPENDED IN A MAGNETIC FIELD WHICH ALLOWS
HEAT/POWER TO BE SUSTAINED WITH LITTLE OR NO ADDITIONAL
POWER. PLEASE GO TO GOOGLE AND ENTER "STELLARATOR" OR VISIT
THE US DEPARTMENT OF ENERGY'S SITE AT PRINCETON UNIVERSITY AT
WWW.PPPL.GOV/NCSX FOR FASCINATING INFORMATION ON THIS
TECHNOLOGY THAT WILL BE OUR FUTURE.

                    LING SUN
          System ready?

Ling nods to Hartwell.

                    PROFESSOR HARTWELL
          One last connection.

Professor clicks one last plug.

                    LING SUN
          Watch the screen Dustin.

The machine turns on. On the MONITOR, a glowing blue plasma
rotates on the screen.

                    DUSTIN
          How's this going to power San Fran?

Ling reads the monitor.

                    LING SUN
          4000 degrees Fahrenheit and stable.

                         JACK
          That'll boil a few cups of water.

Jack tussles Dustin's hair. Dustin is amazed.

                       LING SUN
          Bout time for me to crawl out of
          bed and start cooking dinner.

Dustin looks at Erin puzzled.

Jack walks over to the corner and hands them two WET-SUITS.

                         JACK
          These will fit.

                         ERIN
          Don't look at me.

Ling, Erin and Dustin put on their wet-suits. Ling motions
for the group to follow her.

INT. ROOM UNDERNEATH DOCK

4 PERSONAL UNDERWATER PROPULSION DEVICES float underneath the
dock.

                        DUSTIN
          No way.

                       LING SUN
          Stay close, it's murky under there.

INT. UNDERWATER

Dustin and Erin clad in goggles and respirators follow behind
Ling on their LIGHTED propulsion devices.

They arrive at two posts. Ling motions upward. They arrive
at their boat house. Ling removes her respirator and mask.

                       LING SUN
          You guys wait here.

Ling hurries down a tunnel.

INT. BEDROOM - JACK'S LODGE

Ling enters through a side door. Covered by a sheet, a
MOTORIZED MOVING DUMMY occasionally moves it legs. The TV
BLARES a talk show.

She carefully pulls the dummy back and puts her own legs in its place. She turns off he TV with a remote. She yawns.

> LING SUN
> Ohhh.. Time to start the day.

Ling lunges out of bed toward the bathroom. She pauses at the doorway, slightly pulling down her underwear, spanking her ass for the camera.

INT. CONTROL ROOM

Greeley, bored out of his mind, sees Ling spank her butt and smiles. Roman approaches and erases his smile.

> ROMAN
> Anything new?

> GREELEY
> No sir. Routine day.

> ROMAN
> They must know something.

> GREELEY
> If they did, sir, I'd report it.

> ROMAN
> I protected you in the meeting.

> GREELEY
> I appreciate that sir.

Roman walks away.

Greeley rolls his eyes. Rachel sitting nearby at her monitor smiles at Greeley.

INT. TUNNEL

Ling walks with Dustin and Erin.

> LING SUN
> Whatever you do, stay out of our
> room.

> DUSTIN
> Do they see you guys, you know..

Dustin puts his index finger in his cylindricated palm.

>   LING SUN
> If we're feeling naughty.

Dustin and Erin chuckle and shake their heads.

>   DUSTIN
> When is Jeanine coming?

>   LING SUN
> Dust, she really loves you. She's
> lost without your dad.

EXT. BOAT DOCK PARKING LOT

A local POLICEMAN monitors a tow truck operator hooking up
the beat up DODGE COLT. The truck drives away.

INT. DINING ROOM - JACK'S LODGE

Erin, Dustin, Jack, Ling and Jeanine finish up eating their
beautiful dinner.

>   JEANINE
> Amazing. I'm doing the dishes.

Jeanine hops up to clear the mess.

>   JACK
> Dustin will help. No free lunch
> around here.

Dustin shrugs and helps to clear.

Jeanine attempts to take the dishes from Dustin.

>   JEANINE
> I can take those.

>   DUSTIN
> I'm completely capable.

Dustin continues to the kitchen.

>   JEANINE
> Your dad used to tell me that about
> you.

>   DUSTIN
> Just leave him out of this.

Jeanine starts to cry. Dustin sighs.

                    JEANINE
          Dustin, I know you think I'm some
          stupid gold-digging bimbo.

                    DUSTIN
          I don't think you're stupid.

Jeanine doesn't know what to say.

                    DUSTIN (cont'd)
              Kidding.

Dustin can't be an ass anymore. He gives her a small hug.

                    JEANINE
          I miss him so much. The way he
          smelled. You smell just like him.

                    DUSTIN
          You think so?

Dustin gives her one more hug. He likes the comparison.
Jeanine take a big sniff. A big smile grows on Jack's face as
he notices their embrace.

INT. LIVING ROOM - LATE EVENING

A FIRE roars. Jack and Ling get up and stumble to bed
leaving Jeanine sitting on the couch with her wine glass.

                    JEANINE
          I'm just going to watch the fire
          for a little while.

                    LING SUN
          OK hun, see you in the morning.

Jeanine smiles and watches them leave. She hears their door
close; reaches in to her pocket and pulls out a small DEVICE.
She walks toward the corner of the room near the windows and
scans.

Dustin ambles toward the fridge wearing just his boxers. He
catches Jeanine in his peripheral vision reflecting from the
window. His interest is piqued. He spies on Jeanine
fiddling near the curtains, out of her view. He ducks.

Jeanine sees a reflection in the window and spins around
walking toward the kitchen. Dustin crouches under the
counters and creeps out of the kitchen. He disappears down
the hall.

INT. HALLWAY

He slips in the shadows near the GRANDFATHER CLOCK. Jeanine
slinks down the hallway.

Dustin holds his breath as Jeanine walks right past him. She
analyzes the silence before turning around to go back to the
living room. Dustin lets his breath go and slips down the
hall to his room.

INT. BEDROOM

Dustin carefully closes the door. His finger slips forcing
the door to make a loud CLICK much to the chagrin of Dustin.

INT. LIVING ROOM

Jeanine spins around toward the CLICK, suspecting Dustin's
room. She walks back down the hall.

INT. BEDROOM - JACK'S LODGE

Dustin puts his finger over Erin's mouth.

                    DUSTIN
          Shhh..

Dustin humps the bed to make it SQUEAK.

EXT. HALLWAY

Jeanine listen at the door. She walks away.

INT. BEDROOM - JACK'S LODGE

Dustin lays near Erin and stares at the ceiling.

                    ERIN
          What's the matter?

                    DUSTIN
          I can't fucking believe it.

INT. KITCHEN - MORNING

Dustin sits with Jack. The remnants of breakfast litter the
table. Ling and Jeanine hang out on the deck that overlooks
the tree-filled valley.

                    DUSTIN
          I'm telling you what I saw.

                    JACK
          Gold digger, silver fox fetish,
          loved his big wanker..maybe. Spy,
          no.

                    DUSTIN
          Dude, go ahead and live in your
          dream world.

                    JACK
          Your dad had her investigated front
          and back. He even knows who busted
          her cherry.

                    DUSTIN
          Then explain the dealie she put in
          the corner.

Dustin motions to the corner. Jack is alarmed and looks to
the corner where he discovered the earlier device.

                    JACK
          What dealie?

                    DUSTIN
          Hell if I know.

Dustin storms over to the corner of the room where Jeanine
inserted the device last night.

Ling and Jeanine come in from the deck. Jeanine is alarmed,
but keeps her cool.

                    LING SUN
          Doing a little house keeping.

                    DUSTIN
               (to Jeanine)
          What did you do with it?

                    JEANINE
          With what?

                    DUSTIN
          The little black thing. The
          microphone. Hell, you tell me.

                    JEANINE
          Was it this?

Jeanine produces a small black object.

                         DUSTIN
               What's that?

                         JEANINE
                    (demure)
               A black pearl.

Dustin looks at it.

                         DUSTIN
               That's not it.

                         JEANINE
               Your dad gave it to me on our first
               anniversary.

                         JACK
               You owe Jeanine an apology.

                         DUSTIN
               For what?

Ling finally steps in.

                         LING SUN
               For being so rude.

                         JEANINE
               Was I doing this?

Jeanine walks over to the corner and feigns a yoga move,
ending in a singular stance, similar to what Dustin saw.

                         JEANINE (cont'd)
               My yoga helps me relax.

                         DUSTIN
               That wasn't it and you know it.

                         LING SUN
                    (angrily)
               Dustin.

Dustin storms out of the room.

                         JEANINE
               I'm sorry.

                         JACK
               Kid is going through a lot.

                         JEANINE
               You can't blame him for being
               protective.

                         JACK
          Otto hated being in a fishbowl.

                       JEANINE
          He never explained it all to me.

Jeanine looks at Jack with wide innocent eyes. For the first
time Jack suspects her of lying, but he's baffled.

INT. CONTROL ROOM

Roman approaches Greeley who lists at the blank monitor from
Jack's bedroom.

                         ROMAN
          Why hasn't she installed it!

Greeley shrugs.

                       GREELEY
          I dunno man.

Greeley sits up.

                    GREELEY (cont'd)
          Uh, sir.

Roman storms away. Greeley clicks over to a soccer game on
the same monitor. He makes a "score" motion with his hands
and silently jumps around his area.

INT. LIVING ROOM

Ling comforts Jeanine.

                       JEANINE
          I don't know what I would do
          without you guys.

Jack isn't moved. Ling motions him away. He gladly complies.

                       LING SUN
          You know we're here for you.

                       JEANINE
          I've got to get going.

                       LING SUN
          Will you call me tomorrow?

Jeanine nods.

INT. CONTROL ROOM

Greeley devours the soccer game, with his feet on the desk
and headphones on. Roman approaches and slaps his feet off
the desk.

>   ROMAN
>   They're in the mountains!

>   GREELEY
>   Wha?

>   ROMAN
>   That girl, Erin, her brother's car
>   was towed 2 miles from Jack's
>   house.

>   GREELEY
>   Well he's not at his house.

Greeley clicks over to the bedroom monitor.

>   ROMAN
>   I'm sending my own people up there.

Greeley looks concerned.

INT. TREE TRUNK LABORATORY

Dustin, Jack and Hartwell carefully carry the PROTOTYPE up
the stairs.

>   LING SUN
>   Careful.

EXT. FOREST

The group carefully trods through the forest to a tricked out
FORD EXPEDITION.

EXT. BOAT DOCK PARKING LOT

They load the prototype and jump in.

INT. FORD EXPEDITION

>   ERIN
>   My brother's gonna be pissed.

                    DUSTIN
          We'll buy him 3 just like it.

On a curve, their SUV passes TWO SEDANS, one carrying Roman
and his henchmen.

EXT. PARKING LOT

Roman arrives at the boat dock parking lot. He steps out and
scans the area.

                    ROMAN
               Separate.

Roman motions his 4 henchmen in opposite directions, himself
walking in to the woods.

EXT. MOSCONE CONVENTION CENTER

THE group pulls up to the check in GUARD. Hartwell hands him
his IDENTIFICATION.

A banner above reads: INTERNATIONAL ALTERNATIVE ENERGY
SYMPOSIUM.

                    GUARD
               Your name's Ben Franklin, that's
               cool.

Hartwell nods and smiles. The guard motions down the alley.

                    GUARD (cont'd)
               Alternative fuel cars are located
               on 8 west.

The guard hands him his documents and site MAP.

                    HARTWELL
               Thank you.

Ling grabs the site map from the documents.

                    LING SUN
               Pull in here.

A sign reads 4 EAST.

Another security guard checks their documents.

                    GUARD #2
               Cars are over there.

Ling bats her eyes and flirts.

> LING SUN
> Honey, they're just dropping me
> off.

He waves them in.

INT. ENERGY SYMPOSIUM

Erin distributes FLYERS at break neck pace. Her clean cut
beauty and sweet disposition make her a hit at nerd central.

A couple nerds re-approach her, pointing and commenting on
her flyer, quite fascinated and pleased.

Dustin approaches Erin without disrespecting the nerds.

> DUSTIN
> You about ready for the big show?

> ERIN
> (to nerds)
> Excuse me.

> NERD #1
> I worked on the Stellarator at
> Princeton. You figured it out!

Erin nods and smiles and walks away with Dustin.

> DUSTIN
> Prof's all ready.

Dustin and Erin jump on stage to join the professor who
stands in front of their SUV.

A small sign reads:

> 2:30 DISCUSSION

The professor nervously looks at his watch which reads 2:28.
10 attendees mill about their booth. Erin does her part
innocently flirting and keeping the interest of the
scientists.

A skeptical SCIENTIST (42) sneers at Erin.

> SKEPTIC
> What is this, some new engine that
> runs on farts?

Some of the scientists LAUGH thinking it's the funniest thing
they've ever heard. Erin is speechless and grossed out.

                    PROFESSOR HARTWELL
               Not a bad idea for conservation,
               but...

Professor nods to Erin and Dustin.

                    PROFESSOR HARTWELL (cont'd)
               Let's begin.

Dustin opens the SUV trunk and nods to Erin for assistance.
Together they pull out the prototype and place it on the
large table in front. They turn it on. A blue glowing SHAPE
appears on the monitor.

Most of the attendees interest is piqued.

                    PROFESSOR HARTWELL (cont'd)
               This is the most efficient toroidal
               shape that the plasma can be
               twisted into and suspended in this
               magnetic field.

The group grows.

Erin hands out more FLYERS to the newcomers.

A YOUNG SCIENTIST quickly scans the information.

                    YOUNG SCIENTIST
               These formulas have never been
               proven.

                    PROFESSOR HARTWELL
               If you'll analyze them yourself,
               you'll see that they are now.

The group grows larger. The buzz is unstoppable. The group
beams with victory.

EXT. BOAT DOCK PARKING LOT

Roman tromps out of the woods in frustration. He grabs his
high tech BINOCULARS in his sedan.

ROMAN'S POV: Through infrared, the binoculars pan from the
woods to the water.

Roman is frustrated he clicks over a button.

EXTREME CLOSE UP: A finger switching the INFRARED button to
DAYTIME.

ROMAN'S POV: Roman scans the same area gain.

Roman realizes he saw something on infrared. He switches the
binoculars back.

ROMAN'S POV: The infrared reveals a slightly GLOWING trail
that leads in to the woods.

Roman motions his henchmen to follow.

INT. FOREST

Roman lopes forward following the illuminated pathway of
footsteps. The footsteps end at the REDWOOD TREE. Roman
feels around the tree. He motions his men around the tree,
accidently knocking the BRANCH. The tree opens. Roman and
the men rush in, guns pulled.

INT. TREE TRUNK LABORATORY

Roman kicks equipment around the deserted laboratory.

                    ROMAN
          Damn them!

Roman runs to the area where one UNDERWATER PROPULSION
DEVICES remains.

Roman stops. His mind flashes to the SUV that passed them on
the road. He realizes it's Jack, Hartwell and company, clad
in sunglasses.

                    ROMAN (cont'd)
          Moscone!

Roman immediately calls on his space age phone, as he is
patched through he yells to his men with him.

                    ROMAN (cont'd)
          Burn it all!

INT. MOSCONE CONVENTION CENTER

The area around their SUV is ringed with onlookers, many on
their cell phones.

4 SUNGLASSED MEN synchronously stare towards Professor
Hartwell.

                              HARTWELL
                    Time to go bye-bye.

Hartwell and company immediately leave their exhibit and
struggle through the thick crowd.

The henchmen unsuccessfully attempt to run towards them.
Dustin is the last to exit through the EMERGENCY EXIT. He
pulls the FIRE ALARM, in addition to the SPRINKLER. The BUZZ
is deafening. Conventioneers head to the exit en masse. The
SPRINKLERS kick on and add to the mayhem.

INT. MOSCONE CONVENTION CENTER CORRIDOR

The group runs down the corridor.

                              LING SUN
                    This way.

EXT. MOSCONE CONVENTION CENTER

                              JACK
                    They are all over here.

Ling scans the area noting men in suits talking to
themselves, scanning the area.

                              HOMELESS MAN
                    Spare change?

Ling spins around and notices a GROUP of 5 HOMELESS people
with appropriate signs, and beggar dishes, drunk out of their
minds.

INT. SEDAN

Roman speeds down the road.

                              ROMAN
                    How could you lose them?

EXT. MOSCONE CONVENTION CENTER

                              HENCHMAN
                    Sir, they just vanished.

The henchman turns around in disgust to a HOMELESS PERSON
touching his leg who sits with a group of four similar
persons.

                              HENCHMAN (cont'd)
              Back off!

The crowd continues to stream out of the convention center.
Many soaked to the bone.

                              HENCHMAN (cont'd)
              Not you sir.

The henchman hurries away toward another man in his
organization.

                              DUSTIN
              Oh my God, You stink Erin!

Dustin is the homeless person who grabbed the man's leg.

                              ERIN
              So do you!

Jack, Ling and Professor Hartwell round out the group of
disguised homeless people.

                              DUSTIN
              I'm going to have to start calling
              you "urine".

Jack notices a man exiting a cab at the corner. He motions
the group to run for it. Jack tosses the cabbie a $100 BILL.
The group peels off their CLOTHES, tossing them out the cab
window as it speeds away.

EXT. MOSCONE CONVENTION CENTER

A henchman notices a band of dirty tanned drunk people
dressed in CLEAN STREET CLOTHES. He spins around and runs to
the same area where the man grabbed his leg. He looks in the
street and notices strewn CLOTHES. He runs out in the middle
of the street and kicks them in the air. A car skids to a
stop in front of him and HONKS.

INT. CAB

The cab winds its way down a mountain road filled with Jack
and company. A ROADBLOCK stops the cab.

                              POLICEMAN
              Fire on Suntow ridge...locals only.

The group observes the SMOKE in the distance.

Jack sits in his underwear looking ridiculous.

                         POLICEMAN (cont'd)
              Sorry sir, No entry.

Another officer approaches, smiling.

                         2ND POLICEMAN
              Burning Man is about 3 hours north
              of here.

Jack shakes his head, not wanting to argue.

                         JACK
              Take me to the "stuffed owl".

INT. STUFFED OWL BAR

The group shares a pitcher of beer, now dressed in Army
surplus and hunting clothes in the run-down local bar

ON TV: a hometown newscaster reports.

                         NEWSCASTER
              The Suntow fire has been contained
              to 30 acres, helped by calm breezes
              and--

HONK

                         BARTENDER
              Hey Jack, Clara's here.

                         JACK
              Put it on my account.

The bartender nods. The group rushes out to the truck.

EXT. BAR PARKING LOT

Clara pulls a tarp over the group huddled in the bed of her
truck.

                         CLARA
              There now Jackie, all tucked in.

Clara chuckles and hops in her truck.

EXT. ROADBLOCK

The officers wave Clara through. A henchman waits nearby in
his sedan waiting for the group to arrive at the roadblock.

EXT. DRIVEWAY - JACK'S LODGE

The group waves goodbye to Clara as she backs up the
driveway. They turn and walk in to the home.

INT. CONTROL ROOM

Roman approaches Barry, who now sits at Greeley's computer,
working diligently.

                    ROMAN
          Do a back up and retrieve them.

Barry pounds away. Roman pushes him out of the way and
clicks at the keys himself.

The MONITOR reads: Greeley #679

TESLA FILE: FULL SECURITIZED DELETION: NO RECOVERY

                    ROMAN (cont'd)
          Put a tracer on his implant.

A woman approaches.

                    YOUNG WOMAN
          Sir, they would like to speak with
          you.

She hands Roman a high tech phone.

                    ROMAN
               (subservient)
          Yes...I---

Noticeable YELLING comes out of the earpiece.

                    ROMAN (cont'd)
          Sir, this was out of my control.

The YELLING continues.

                    ROMAN (cont'd)
          I was just notified of Greeley.

                    BARRY
          Sir, he's on the Golden Gate
          Bridge.

Barry pushes buttons which then show and AERIAL SATELLITE
VIEW of San Francisco. A white BEEP flashes on the center of
the Golden Gate Bridge.

                    ROMAN
          Tell our men on the bridge.

Barry runs down the hall.

EXT. GOLDEN GATE BRIDGE

Greeley folds a SWISS ARMY KNIFE. He holds his bleeding wound
near his tricep. He is dressed like a Haight-Ashbury street
rasta. He throws the micro IMPLANT off the Bridge.

GREELEY's P.O.V.

Two men from his organization run towards Greeley on the
crowded bridge. One holds a black GLOBAL POSITIONING
LOCATOR.

The men race past Greeley as he saunters away with a groove
in his step. Greeley remains cool as a cucumber observing the
men looking over the bridge railing.

One of the men speaks in to his collar.

INT. CONTROL ROOM

Barry touches his earpiece.

                    BARRY
          Sir, he's killed himself. It's
          beeping in the bay.

Roman spins to Barry.

                    ROMAN
          Tell 49 to be ready in two hours.
          I can't complete this without her.
          They will be running to Jack for
          comfort.

EXT. GOLDEN GATE BRIDGE

Two stereotypical tourists, complete with Bermuda shorts and
dangling CAMERA, saunter by the men.

                    HENCHMAN
               (to tourists)
          Did you see anyone jump?

                    TOURIST
          Are you shitting me? Sheila, did
          you hear that?

The tourist motions for his plump girlfriend to look over the
side with him.

                    TOURIST (cont'd)
          Can you believe it? Right here in
          front of us baby! First two men
          kissing in the park, and now this!
          Get that man to get a picture of us
          standing here.

The MEN are stunned and take the camera from him and comply.

INT. CONTROL ROOM

Raquel looks over her shoulder and begins typing furiously.

                    RAQUEL
               (to herself)
          Greeley...

The computer shows the transfer of $4,999,999. to an account
at BANK OF SWITZERLAND in the name of Jim Morrison, Jr.

Raquel shakes her head, obviously sad.

Her cordless headset beeps. She is startled.

                    RAQUEL (cont'd)
          Yes Roman, how can I be of service?

INT. ROMAN'S SEDAN

Roman and Barry speed in the Mountains.

                    ROMAN
          Where have you been!

                    RAQUEL
          I...I was in the bathr--

INTERCUT AS NEEDED

                    ROMAN
          Where's 49?

Raquel clicks her keyboard.

                        RAQUEL
            Sir, I show her just about to
            arrive.

ON MONITOR: An AERIAL VIEW from 400 ft. of a car winding up a
mountain road.

                        ROMAN
            Connect me with her, now!

                        RAQUEL
            Yes sir.

Raquel pushes a special handset.

                        RAQUEL (cont'd)
            Umm, Jeanine, it's Raquel.

INT. JEANINE'S PORSCHE

                        JEANINE
                    (happily excited)
            Raquel! Greeley told--!

Raquel interrupts.

                        RAQUEL
            Yes Jeanine, he's gone. I have
            Roman on the line.

INTERCUT AS NEEDED

                        JEANINE
            Hello Roman.

                        ROMAN
            Jeanine, is that what we're calling
            you now? We're taking them out
            tonight.

                        JEANINE
            It's not necessary.

                        ROMAN
            Not necessary! My ass is on the
            line. If I hadn't listened to you.

INT. JACK'S LODGE - EVENING

The DOORBELL rings. Jack looks up to the door TV MONITOR and
notices Jeanine. He jerks open the large door, looks around
and nervously pulls her inside.

                         JACK
          Well, look what the cat dragged in.
          I thought you weren't coming until
          tomorrow?

                         JEANINE
          Sorry, I just couldn't wait after
          all that happened.

Ling hops over to give Jeanine a heartfelt hug and welcomes
her.

Jeanine goes right for Dustin who is now finally glad to see
her.

                         JEANINE (cont'd)
          I was so scared.

Dustin just nods.

                         JACK
          It's good to see you two finally
          getting along.

Jeanine gives Erin a quick hug.

                         JEANINE
          So good to see you too.

Jeanine is obviously pensive, and observes the candlelit
room. She looks like she might blurt out whatever is on her
mind, and looks around the room to CAMERAS she knows she has
hidden in the past.

Ling approaches with a glass of wine.

                         LING SUN
          We're trying to be a little
          incognito.

Jeanine can't stand it any longer.

                         JEANINE
          Dustin, could I speak with you for
          a moment.

                         DUSTIN
          Sure. But we're cool now.

Dustin gets up to follow Jeanine out to the deck. Dustin
closes the door behind her.

Jeanine looks out to the dark forest. Dustin stands near her
and looks out. He realizes she's been crying.

                    JEANINE
          You know. When I was young, I was
          pretty jaded.

                    DUSTIN
          Worse than me?

                    JEANINE
          I never thought I would find love.
          Until they sent me to your father.

                    DUSTIN
          What?

                    JEANINE
          You were right about me?

                    DUSTIN
          Which part? I don't care if you
          were bonking him for his money?

                    JEANINE
          My meeting your father was no
          accident.

                    DUSTIN
          Whadya mean?

                    JEANINE
          I'm going to take care of them, at
          least for now. We need to change
          your identities. You need to go in
          to hiding.

                    DUSTIN
          I'm not hiding from anyone.
          Them... What a bunch of pussies.
          Who's them?!

Jeanine pulls him closer to quiet him. He pushes her away.

Just then Erin thoughtlessly flips on the kitchen LIGHT. The
room illuminates silhouetting Dustin and Jeanine against the
glass. Jack jumps over and flicks off the light.

A red LASER flickers off the glass window. Jeanine panics
and pushes Dustin down with brute strength.

                    DUSTIN (cont'd)
          What the fuck are you doing?

Dustin is freaked by her strength. Just at that moment the
glass door SHATTERS sending glass everywhere.

Ling and Jack are alerted. Erin already hides on the kitchen
floor shaking.

                    JACK
          Everybody downstairs. We're taking
          the tunnel.

They crouch low and head to downstairs.

                    JEANINE
          That's the first place they'll
          look.

                    JACK
          It's a secret.

                    JEANINE
          Built in 1978, 114 feet long, 3
          foot walls, who do you think was
          the winning contractor?

Jack is furious.

                    JACK
          How could you stay in my house
          and...and drink my WINE. If--

                    JEANINE
          Four are waiting.

                    LING SUN
          Jack, she's on our side now.

Jack stands up and looks outside. The red LASER appears on
his forehead. Jeanine pulls him down. A bullet WHIZZES by
and embeds in a wall.

Jack realizes her importance.

                    JACK
          I'm not going down without a fight.

Jack scrambles to his gun cabinet and pushes in the code.
The door pops open. He slides pistols and ammunition down to
the crouching group.

                    ERIN
          I've never shot a gun.

                    JACK
          You just point and shoot. Just
          like a camera.

Erin is panicked. Dustin gazes at her and gives her a kiss.

                         DUSTIN
             I got you in this, and I'm going to
             get you out.

Erin kisses him back.

                         JEANINE
             They've got infrared, and more.

                         JACK
             And so do I.

Jack scrambles back to his gun rack and retrieves 2 pairs of
INFRARED GOGGLES.

                         DUSTIN
             Why'd you have these?

                         JACK
             Ling and I used to play hide and go
             seek outside before we'd...oh,
             never mind.

Dustin smiles and takes a pair.

                         JEANINE
             I'll take the front.

Jeanine takes Dustin's baseball cap off his head and starts
ramming her long hair underneath the cap.

Dustin appreciates her authority.

                         JACK
             There's four trails that lead out
             of here.

Jack sidles up to the TV monitors near the hallway. He
pushes EXTERIOR TREES button. He pushes the button
NIGHTTIME.

                         JACK (cont'd)
             You were right about the tunnel.

ON MONITOR: A henchman appears through the greenish hue.

Jack pushes another button.

                         JACK (cont'd)
             That's the easiest trail.

ON MONITOR: Another of Roman's men appears.

                    JEANINE
          Roman's on his way.

                    JACK
          Who's he?

                    JEANINE
          The man who has been hounding you
          for 20 years.

Jack pushes another button.

ON MONITOR: Barry appears.

                    JEANINE (cont'd)
          He's here.

Jeanine reaches to a small device and speaks in to it.

                    JEANINE (cont'd)
          Roman, what's your location?

                    ROMAN (O.S.)
          Jeanine, where are you!?

                    JEANINE
          I have them hidden in the wine
          cellar. Tell me where you are?

                    ROMAN (O.S.)
          Why did you save Dustin?

                    JEANINE
          You want them all don't you?

                    ROMAN (O.S.)
          I'm on the upper driveway.

                    JEANINE
          Come to the back door downstairs,
          and they are all yours. Tell the
          others to follow. We need to do
          this quickly.

Dustin holds his hands out wondering her plan.

Jeanine puts her finger over her mouth. She makes sure
Dustin, Ling and Erin each have a GUN. She motions them in
to Dustin's room upstairs.

                    JEANINE (cont'd)
          If I'm not back in 5 minutes,
          scatter in the woods.

The group enters Dustin's room.

INT. DUSTIN'S ROOM

The group sits huddled on the bed. Dustin comforts terrified Erin.

INT. DOWNSTAIRS HALLWAY

Jeanine, with gun in hand, opens the framed glass door motioning Roman and Barry inside.

> JEANINE
> Where are the other two?

> ROMAN
> Securing upstairs.

Jeanine is panic stricken but keeps her cool.

> JEANINE
> They are in there.

Jeanine motions to the wine cellar door.

> JEANINE (cont'd)
> Make it clean.

> ROMAN
> Good work forty,..Jeanine.

Jeanine hears the DOOR OPENING upstairs. She opens the wine door.

> JEANINE
> Behind the cases in the back.

Jeanine motions. Roman and Barry enter. She slams the heavy door and spins the lock on the cellar door, setting the lock for 12 days.

INT. CELLAR

Roman realizes he's been had. He starts SHOOTING at the metal door, to no avail.

INT. DOWNSTAIRS HALLWAY

Jeanine sees the third man standing near the glass door. She opens the door.

                         MAN #3
                 Is it over?

She makes a "Shhhhh" motions and whispers in his ear, holding
the gun to his head.

                         JEANINE
                 Didn't we have martial arts
                 together?

Jeanine fires her SILENCER. She grabs his lifeless body and
places it on the ground.

                         JEANINE (cont'd)
                 Sorry.

INT. CELLAR

Roman frantically moves about the room, trying to find an
escape. Barry attempts to make radio contact.

                         MAN #1
                 Lead walls sir, no signal.

Roman kicks a case of expensive wine to the ground.

He notices an AIR DUCT.

                         ROMAN
                 Has to lead to the outside.

Roman rips off the vent and peers down the duct.

                         ROMAN (cont'd)
                 Hand me that.

Roman motions to a CROWBAR resting on an open wooden case
filled with straw.

With both hands, Roman rams the crowbar to the upper part of
the duct, nothing is moving. Roman is getting exhausted.

Barry takes the crowbar from exhausted Roman.

INT. DUSTIN'S ROOM

The group is frazzled. Erin examines her gun like a foreign
object. The door opens.

                         ERIN
                 Jeanine?

The door opens to reveal MAN #3 shocked to find them there.
Erin SCREAMS, startling the man, and in turn dropping her own
gun. The gun FIRES.

The man drops dead.

Erin runs to his aid.

                    ERIN (cont'd)
          Oh my God, I'm so sorry.

Erin holds her hand to her mouth. MAN #3 has a bullet in his
head, his eyes wide open.

Jeanine runs to the room.

                    JEANINE
          Nice work.

Jeanine comforts freaked out Erin. The group hears wild
BANGING.

                    JEANINE (cont'd)
          They are locked in tight for 12
          days. That should give us plenty
          of time to figure out--

The BANGING becomes more pronounced. The sound of wood
CRACKING. The group runs to the office where they notice a
CROWBAR poking through the floor, then being pulled back.
Bullets WHIZ straight up to the ceiling.

                    JACK
          The vent!

                    JEANINE
          Everybody in the car.

INT. CELLAR

Roman holds his space-age phone up to the hole and cranes his
head to its microphone.

                    ROMAN
          Freeze radio waves on my position!

INT. BLACK SUBURBAN

Jack backs the Suburban out of the 6 car garage. The
automatic car door locks click UP and DOWN several times.
The radio flashes ENTER SECURITY CODE.

                         JEANINE
                    He's out! GO!

INT. CELLAR

Roman and Barry thrust the door open. Roman nods. They both
take out strange-looking GUNS with thin long muzzles. They
point to opposite walls. FLAMES shoot out, igniting the
walls. They run up the stairs.

INT. LIVING ROOM

Roman and Barry TORCH the living room and hallway.

EXT. DRIVEWAY

Roman looks up the long driveway noticing their black
suburban SQUEALING out of sight.

INT. BLACK SUBURBAN

Jack rolls down his window. He FIRES, blowing two tires out
of Roman's Mercedes, HISS, HISS. He fires at the passenger
window. The bullet bounces off.

EXT. DRIVEWAY

Roman runs up the driveway towards his car. He finds the
flattened tires. He pushes the security lock to open the
door. Both jump in the car.

INT. ROMAN'S MERCEDES

Roman opens a panel behind the radio revealing several
buttons. He pushes a series of BUTTONS.

EXT. ROMAN'S MERCEDES

The tires reinflate.

INT. ROMAN'S MERCEDES

Roman spies the Suburban's tail lights in the distance down
the winding road. Roman picks up his phone.

                    ROMAN
          Need back up.

Barry works a GPS MONITOR on the middle dash.

                    ROMAN (cont'd)
          Both dead. How long for
          assistance?

Roman overtakes and scans the GPS MONITOR. Roman slams the
phone down and speeds toward the taillights.

                    ROMAN (cont'd)
          We're taking care of this alone.

INT. CHEVY TRUCK

Clara Johnson grabs a CAN OF COPENHAGEN and readies her lip
for a dip. After she places a large wad in her front lip she
takes a sip from a PINT Whiskey bottle. Her AM RADIO plays
twangy COUNTRY MUSIC.

She looks up to notice Jack's Suburban race by.

                    CLARA
               (singing)
          "You gotta stop, and smell the
          roses, you gotta count your many
          blessings everyday..a,uh,yeah..

Clara pulls out in the direction of the Suburban and spits
out the window.

INT. BLACK SUBURBAN

IN REAR VIEW MIRROR: Jack's attention is caught by the glare
of Clara's headlights.

Dustin jerks around to the lights.

                    DUSTIN
          Is that them?

Jack takes a long look.

                    JACK
          Nope, that's our Clara out for her
          evening drive.

Jack is a bit relieved until he sees the Mercedes headlights
barreling down on Clara.

INT. CHEVY TRUCK

Clara notices the Mercedes riding her tail.

                    CLARA
          Aw, it's you again!

Roman's attempts to pass her. Clara swerves in his path.

INT. ROMAN'S MERCEDES

Roman is confounded.

                    ROMAN
          Take her out.

Barry leans out the car window, takes aim and FIRES through
her back window.

INT. CHEVY TRUCK

The bullet SHATTERS her rear window, startling the hell out
of Clara.

                    CLARA
          Now you're gonna git it.

Clara reaches under her seat for a sawed off SHOTGUN. She
deftly cocks it with one hand and places the muzzle through
the missing window. She fires two shots without looking.

INT. ROMAN'S MERCEDES

The bullets RICOCHET off his bullet-proof windshield, right
in front of his head. Roman is startled, yet determined.

INT. BLACK SUBURBAN

Jack pulls a sharp right up the small hidden road towards the
helicopter.

INT. CHEVY TRUCK

Clara stomps on her brakes.

INT. ROMAN'S MERCEDES

Roman SLAMS his car in to the rear of the Chevy truck,
forcing Barry to drop his gun out the window. Roman glances
over to his blunder.

                    ROMAN
          Damnit!

Barry grabs another gun. He aims at Clara's rear tires and
FIRES. The tires EXPLODE.

INT. CHEVY TRUCK

Clara starts to lose control of her truck. She runs in to a
ditch, bumping her head.

                    CLARA
          Those were fresh re-treads!

She bangs the steering wheel.

Roman races by in his sedan. Clara hurls her half empty
whiskey PINT at the car like a trained knife thrower.

INT. ROMAN'S MERCEDES

The whiskey PINT clunks Barry in the head. Barry holds his
now bleeding temple and MOANS.

Roman can't believe Clara's skill.

EXT. HILLSIDE NEAR HELICOPTER PAD

Jack speeds up the hill. He pushes his remote, opening the
electric gate.

INT. ROMAN'S MERCEDES

Roman examines the dashboard GPS. A LIGHT flashes off the
main road grid. Baffled, he races by the entrance of the
road. He stomps on the brakes. He jams the car in REVERSE
and peels rubber backwards, finding the almost invisible
entrance. Roman CRASHES through the gate.

EXT. HELICOPTER PAD

Jack runs to the helicopter first and hops in.

INT. HELICOPTER

Jack flips all the necessary switches and flips the ignition.
The blades slowly WHIR and start. Jack hops out to assist
the others.

EXT. HILLSIDE NEAR HELICOPTER PAD

Dustin assists Erin and Jeanine out of the Suburban.

                    JACK
          Go! Go! GO!

Jack grabs Ling and runs her to the side door of the
helicopter and hurries her inside.

Erin approaches first, Jack shoves her inside.

Jack notices the flash of headlights reflecting off the tree.

                    JACK (cont'd)
          Get in the BIRD!

Dustin turns around and notices the headlights.

Jack takes his GUN and starts firing. The bullets bounce off
like raindrops on a well-waxed car.

The Mercedes slides to a stop on the gravel.

INT. MERCEDES

Barry jerks open his door and fires at Dustin. He misses.
Dustin crouches.

EXT. HILLSIDE NEAR HELICOPTER PAD

Jack bravely takes aim at Barry, hitting him in the face,
killing him.

                    JACK
          Get in Dustin, I've got him!

Jack fires at Roman hiding in the Mercedes.

Roman cowardly sticks his GUN only outside his window and
fires just above Dustin's head who attempts to enter the
helicopter.

Dustin ducks down, Erin and Ling SCREAM.

                         LING SUN
                  Jack, GET IN!

Jack jumps in the copter.

Jeanine grasps the helicopter door handle and opens it. She
creates a human shield as she SHOVES Dustin inside the
copter.

Two bullets RIP through her torso. She lets out a GASP.

Jack jumps halfway out and rapid fires at Roman keeping him
inside the Mercedes.

Jeanine's eyes are fixed on Dustin.

Dustin grabs Jeanine to try to pull her in, there is limited
room. She is obviously dying. Dustin has tears and fear in
his eyes.

Jack jumps back in.

                         DUSTIN
                  Oh, Jeanine.

                         JEANINE
                  Make your father proud.

Another BULLET hits Jeanine. She slumps out of his arms.
Dustin lets her go.

INT. HELICOPTER

Dustin puts his face in his hands. Jack jerks the YOKE to
ready for lift off.

EXT. HELICOPTER PAD

Roman rushes towards the helicopter as it lifts off.

He grabs the helicopter's landing gear SKID on Dustin's side.

Jack lifts off.

INT. HELICOPTER

Dustin notices Roman hanging on. Jack realizes the weight
imbalance and struggles to right the helicopter.

EXT. HELICOPTER

Roman holds on for dear life and tries to point his gun
toward the passenger cabin. The wild ROCKING makes this
impossible for him to get a shot.

INT. HELICOPTER

Jack barely clears the trees.

                    JACK
               (yelling)
          Ever see a dog with poo stuck to
          it's butt?

Jack purposely scrapes the tops of the trees.

Roman pulls his legs up and secures himself on the skid.

Jack can't believe his eyes when he notices his home is
ABLAZE. He is devastated, hurt and sad. Ling looks at him,
trying to comfort him. She puts her hand on his shoulder.

He flies right over the burning home and HOVERS.

                    JACK (cont'd)
          Hold on to your hats.

Jack begins wild acrobatics over the BURNING HOUSE.

EXT. HELICOPTER

Roman's legs slip off the skid. He holds on with only his
arms, attempting to gain a better grip. He manages to get a
leg up, and pulls out his gun and attempts to fire.

Jack wildly jerks the helicopter. Roman loses his grip.
With both hands, he FIRES his gun three times as he falls in
to the FIERY BUILDING.

A CLOSE UP reveals the bullet puncturing the transmission oil
storage near the blade.

INT. HELICOPTER

Ling and Erin hug each other. Dustin turns around and
aggressively pulls Erin to him, kissing her passionately. He
then pats Jack on the back.

                    DUSTIN
          Nice work captain.

Ling reaches around and gives a quick kiss to Jack.

> LING SUN
> You wanted to remodel anyway,
> remember?

> JACK
> Aw, now.

Jack taps the oil pressure gauge steadily dropping. A warning
BUZZER SOUNDS.

Oil drips on the windshield.

> JACK (cont'd)
> We're going down kids.

Ling and Erin are terrified.

Jack maneuvers the helicopter towards a pitch black area in
the distance. The helicopter starts to yaw.

> JACK (cont'd)
> Got your swimsuits on?

Amid the warning BUZZERS, Jack expertly guides the helicopter
over the water, and hovers.

> JACK (cont'd)
> End of the line.

> LING SUN
> I can't leave you!

> JACK
> Git going woman.

Jack opens his door.

> JACK (cont'd)
> You better take her with you.

Ling takes Erin's hand. The helicopter loses power and yaws
more. The two step down to the skid, nod and jump in to the
black.

> DUSTIN
> I'm staying with you.

> JACK
> You're doing no such thing.

Jack points and demands he exit.

                         JACK (cont'd)
          Better go now or Erin's going to
          end up with a few dents in her
          head.

                         DUSTIN
          I love you Jack.

Dustin looks straight in his eyes, turns and jumps.

Jack struggles to ensure the helicopter flies straight away
from the group. The BLADES freeze. The helicopter drops
straight towards the water. KERSPLASH!

EXT. LAKE

Ling and Erin struggle to tread water. Erin gasps for breath
from the shock. Dustin swims toward her and attempts to calm
her. Ling closes her eyes watching the helicopter crash.

                         LING SUN
          Come on Jack.

The group swims rapidly towards the wreckage.

                         DUSTIN
          JACK! JACK!

Ling races at Olympic pace ahead of the two.

                         DUSTIN (cont'd)
          JACK!

Ling stays on her course. A HAND grabs Ling, stopping her
stride.

                         JACK
          You got a nice stroke there kid.

Jack and Ling kiss and squeeze each other.

                         JACK (cont'd)
          Watch the shoulder.

Dustin is not far behind. He reaches the two. Dustin hugs
Jack.

                         JACK (cont'd)
          You're gonna drown me boy.

Erin finally reaches the group.

                    JACK (cont'd)
          Why you guys swimming this way?
          The shore is thatta way.

Jack points towards the FIRE in the distance. Emergency
LIGHTS rotate near the blaze.

Ling splashes water toward him. He begins a one-arm
backstroke toward the shore.

                    JACK (cont'd)
               (singing)
          "Moon River....wider than a mile.
          Two drifters off to see the world"

INT. PROFESSOR HARTWELL'S OFFICE

Professor Hartwell stands hugging Erin and Dustin. A
newspaper headline reads: 24 FUSION GENERATORS SLATED FOR
IMMEDIATE CONSTRUCTION. The professor beams.

                    PROFESSOR HARTWELL
          It's bigger than us now.

Professor Hartwell winks and tussles Dustin's hair.

EXT. ITALIAN RIVIERA

Elegant beach chairs line up in a row. Dustin and Erin sun
themselves clad in Luxoticca glasses on two chaises lounges.

A smartly dressed WAITER delivers Campari and Soda.

A young handsome man in a baseball cap trots up next to
Dustin and drops his satchel on a chaise.

                    GREELEY
          Hey, did you go to Berkeley?

Dustin nods and gets up to shake his hand wondering why he
looks so familiar.

INT. CONTROL ROOM

Raquel works at her computer screen. From satellite distance,
she ZOOMS in on Dustin and Greeley chatting it up at the
beach. She puts her hand on her chin, shakes her head and
smiles. She notices someone approaching her from behind.
She switches the screen to BLACK.

                                        FADE OUT:

www.ingramcontent.com/pod-product-compliance
Lightning Source LLC
Chambersburg PA
CBHW080837250626
47160CB00009B/2972